W9-BRW-813

HOWE
LIBRARY

Travels in Cuba

BY Marie-Louise Gay
AND David Homel

GROUNDWOOD BOOKS
HOUSE OF ANANSI PRESS
TORONTO / BERKELEY

Groundwood Books / House of Anansi Press
groundwoodbooks.com

Groundwood Books respectfully acknowledges that the land on which we operate is the Traditional Territory of many Nations, including the Anishinabeg, the Wendat and the Haudenosaunee. It is also the Treaty Lands of the Mississaugas of the Credit.

Canada Council for the Arts   Conseil des Arts du Canada

With the participation of the Government of Canada
Avec la participation du gouvernement du Canada | Canadä

Library and Archives Canada Cataloguing in Publication
Title: Travels in Cuba / by Marie-Louise Gay and David Homel.
Names: Gay, Marie-Louise, author, illustrator. | Homel, David, author.
Description: Illustrations by Marie-Louise Gay.
Identifiers: Canadiana (print) 20200299565 | Canadiana (ebook) 2020029959X |
ISBN 9781773063478
(hardcover) | ISBN 9781773063485 (EPUB) | ISBN 9781773063492 (Kindle)
Classification: LCC PS8563.A868 T73 2021 | DDC jC813/.54—dc23

Groundwood Books is a Global Certified Accessible™ (GCA by Benetech) publisher. An ebook version of this book that meets stringent accessibility standards is available to students and readers with print disabilities.

Groundwood Books is committed to protecting our natural environment. As part of our efforts, this book is made of material from well-managed FSC®-certified forests, recycled materials and other controlled sources.

Jacket illustration by Marie-Louise Gay
Design by Michael Solomon
Printed and bound in Canada

For children building bridges all around the world

My Adventures

ONE
Batman Comes to Cuba

I was riding a giant roller coaster. It went shooting up hills and hurtled down into valleys at breakneck speed. It lurched from side to side and whizzed around corners.

People were screaming. Their mouths were open so wide I could see their tonsils. Their hair stood on end.

I was screaming, too, when a tremendous thunderclap woke me up.

Our airplane was diving through the clouds. The cabin lights flickered. The seatbelt sign was flashing like the lights on a police car. The doors to some of the overhead bins fell open, and jackets, sun hats, backpacks and a teddy bear flew out.

Some people were crying. Others were gasping for air.

Even the flight attendants looked worried.

I peeked out the window. Lightning flashed from cloud to cloud.

Had we flown into a hurricane? Was I going to die on the first day of my vacation?

Through the uproar, the pilot's voice came on.

"*Señoras y señores*, ladies and gentlemen, we are flying through some uncomfortable air. Please excuse the small turbulence."

Small turbulence? She must be kidding.

I looked across the aisle at my father. He was as white as a mushroom. He was gripping the armrests of his seat, his eyes shut tight. My mother's face was all wrinkled up, like she was trying to imagine she was somewhere else.

Next to me, Max began to pull everything out of his backpack. His stuffed penguin, his comic books, his flashlight, a banana, his underwear — you name it.

At the very bottom of his pack, he found what he was looking for.

His Batman mask. He put it on and smiled.

"Batman to the rescue!" he yelled.

My little brother can get the weirdest ideas. He

probably thought he could save the plane by looking like a superhero. Max is always very helpful in dangerous situations.

All of a sudden, like night and day, the sky outside changed. And the plane stopped shaking. The flight attendants went up and down the aisles, picking up the luggage that had fallen from the bins. They gathered up the burp bags from the passengers who had used them.

I looked out the window again. The black clouds had disappeared, and the sun was shining on a green island shaped like a crocodile floating on a turquoise sea.

We had survived. Our vacation was about to begin.

The pilot's voice came on the speakers.

"Thank you for your patience. We will be landing shortly at the José Martí International Airport in La Habana. *Bienvenidos a Cuba!*"

— • —

After picking up our bags, we walked to the passport control. The officer looked at our passports. Then he looked at us. Then he looked at the pictures on the passports again.

He pointed at Max, his black eyebrows bunching up in a frown under his official cap.

"Quién es?" he barked. "Who is this?"

Max hid behind my mother.

"This is our son Max," said my mother.

"He doesn't look like a Max. He looks like a Batman!" The customs man burst out laughing. *"Batman en Cuba, increíble!* I think maybe we need him here."

Everyone in the line was staring at us.

Sometimes Max can be so embarrassing that I pretend he isn't my brother.

We hurried out of the airport terminal and stood on the sidewalk. Every few seconds, a man would come up to us and shout "Taxi!" very loudly in our faces.

We did not need a taxi. Someone was supposed to be waiting to drive us to where we were staying. But how would we recognize the person?

Then I caught sight of a tall brown man with a huge mustache that hung like a pair of curtains on both sides of his mouth. He was leaning against a car, holding up a sign with our names on it. His car was older than he was, and you could practically see through it, it had so many holes from rust.

My father saw him, too.

"Buenos días," he said to him.

The man grabbed my father's hand and shook it really hard.

"Soy Ledesma, buenos días."

"Buenos días," my father repeated, as Ledesma

went on squishing his hand. *"Buenos días, buenos días."*

My father was stuck on repeat.

Finally, he turned around to me.

"Uh… Charlie?"

I was learning Spanish in school, and I had a few classmates from Mexico.

The first thing you find out when you try to learn a foreign language is that you can't be afraid to make mistakes. I made one mistake for every word I said, but that didn't matter. I found out what I needed to know.

This man named Ledesma with the walrus mustache was going to drive us to Señora Gloria's house, where we would be staying.

"Yes, Señora Gloria, that's it, that's where we're going!" my mother said, very excited, as if we had all just been saved from drowning.

Ledesma took the suitcase out of my father's hand. He might have been older than my father, but he had hands of steel. He held the heavy bag with just two fingers.

"Okay, muchachos," he said to us. Then he bowed to my mother. "And the señora, too."

My father patted the car delicately, so it would not collapse into a heap of rusty metal flakes.

"It's a Lada," he said. "A Russian car."

I had never been in a Russian car before. I wondered how this one had ended up on an island in the middle of the Caribbean Sea.

We all piled in. Ledesma insisted that my mother sit in front. That must have been the most comfortable spot. In the back, the seat was so low I felt like I was sitting on the street.

My mother patted the orange fur that covered the dashboard, just the way she does with our cat, Miro.

"Lion," said Ledesma, stroking it.

He gave a great big laugh. Then he looked at

Max in the rearview mirror and shouted, "Hey, Batman in Cuba!"

Before we drove away, Ledesma reached out, grabbed hold of the small black statue that was hanging from the mirror and kissed it. Maybe that was what you did when you drove a Russian car, or a Russian car with holes in the side.

Then he pulled into the traffic behind a dump truck that was shooting out so much black smoke it looked like it was on fire.

Maybe Max had the right idea with his mask.

My mother was staring at the spider web of cracks in the windshield. She was probably wondering if it was going to end up in her lap.

Meanwhile, Ledesma was talking to her at a hundred miles an hour. I could not hear what he was saying, since we were sitting in back with the windows open. My mother smiled and nodded, which is what you do when you don't understand what someone is saying.

After a while, Ledesma must have gotten tired of the one-way conversation. He turned on the radio, and loud music poured out. It was dance music, but the only thing dancing was the car, jumping up and down over the bumps and rolling from side to side like a ship in a storm.

He talked very fast, but Ledesma was the most relaxed driver I had ever seen. In Montreal, where

I live, everyone is always in a rush. Our drivers will go through red lights if they think they can get away with it, and they cut off other cars for sport.

Not Ledesma. He sang along with the radio, one hand on the steering wheel, the other hanging out the window, tapping the side of the door to the beat.

It looked like Cuba was frozen in the past. The other cars on the road were pretty much like Ledesma's: rusty Russian Ladas or old-time models like the ones you see in black-and-white movies. You know, with big grills in front like shark's teeth, and pointy fins in the back. They were painted bright colors — pink and turquoise and lime green. The city of Havana was like an old-car museum.

There was another thing missing. I didn't see any billboards with ads for clothes or the latest album by some rock star. And no fast-food restaurants, the way there are back home.

But I did see an enormous poster on the side of a building with the picture of a man looking very heroic. He had long hair, a beard and a beret — not the way a soldier or a president would usually be dressed. He was speaking to a giant crowd of people who were all cheering.

"Who's that guy on the poster?" I asked my father.

"Che Guevara."

"Sí, sí," Ledesma said very enthusiastically from the front. "*El Che. Un grande.* Hero of the Revolution. *Viva la Revolución!*"

"Who's Che Guevara?" I asked.

"He helped with the Cuban revolution that threw out a dictator named Batista," my father said. "Everyone loves Che Guevara here, even if he wasn't Cuban. He came from Argentina. Get used to seeing him. He's everywhere."

Ledesma turned up the radio. "La Bamba" poured out of the speaker, and he sang along with it. *"Para bailar la bamba, se necesita una poca de gracia…"* It must have been his favorite song.

Even with the music and the bouncing backseat, my eyes were closing.

Che Guevara would have to wait.

TWO
The Hairless Purple Dog

I opened my eyes and saw two wrecks. A wrecked building and a wrecked car. Ledesma's Lada might have been a little rusty and the seats saggy, but it had delivered us to where we would be staying.

Unfortunately for us.

"Your friend Señora Gloria lives here?" I asked my mother.

An old car with no tires or windshield sat in front of a building that must have been ten stories tall. Our Lada looked like a Rolls-Royce next to the wrecked auto. A man was sitting on an upside-down garbage can in front of the hood, eating. Three very dirty, mangy-looking cats followed his spoon from his plate of rice and beans to his mouth and back again, like they were watching a tennis game.

He had spread out his dinner on a newspaper draped over the hood.

At least the car was still good for something.

"Hola!" Ledesma called to the man. *"Buen provecho!"*

The man raised his spoon as Ledesma got out of the car and walked around a big pile of stones and

rocks to the front of the building. Then he put his hands around his mouth and shouted into the air.

"Gloria! *Mi corazón! Mi vida!*"

My heart? My life? Was he going to have a heart attack, or was he reciting a poem?

The next minute, from a balcony five floors up, a woman's head appeared. Even from the ground, I could see she was wearing a big smile.

"Ledesma, *amor*!" she called.

Then they had some more shouted conversation separated by five stories. I did not catch any of it.

But they must have decided something, because Ledesma walked back to the car, grabbed the heavy suitcase from the trunk and motioned us to follow. I never saw a man that old move so fast.

We picked up our backpacks and ran after him into the lobby of the building.

You know that expression, when something has seen better days? This building had seen better days, but I couldn't tell exactly when those days were. The mailboxes were all broken, there was a pile of old papers in one corner, and some sand in the other.

Ledesma pointed to a metal grill in the wall. It looked like the door to a jail cell.

Were we going to spend our vacation in prison?

"El elevador," he said.

You could have fooled me. Ledesma pulled up

the grill and we all squeezed onto the platform. The *elevador* slowly creaked up into the darkness. It was like being in a horror movie. I could barely see the floors we were passing.

I wondered about the kind of place we were going to stay in, and I bet my parents were wondering the same thing.

I was still wondering as we stumbled down the dark hallway on the fifth floor.

Then everything changed.

The door opened and Señora Gloria appeared. She threw her arms around us, kissed us until it hurt, called Ledesma all sorts of cute names that I would never say in a million years and pushed us into the living room.

The outside of the apartment and the inside were like night and day. The rooms were very big and full of sunlight and flowers and all sorts of souvenirs and pictures. There was even a photograph of Señora Gloria with a man who looked a lot like the heroic guy on the enormous poster. They had their arms around each other, and they were giving the V for Victory sign.

We dropped our bags, happy to finally be somewhere. We were not going to stay in a ruin with wrecked cars and piles of gravel and mangy cats after all.

I walked onto the balcony. There was a beautiful

view of the sea. In front of me stood a palace made of white stone surrounded by green lawns.

It was very strange. Our building looked like it was falling apart, but there was a palace next door.

Señora Gloria showed us to our rooms as she talked at top speed. Her words whirled around me, and I tried to catch up to them.

My parents looked stunned. My mother's eyes were red from not enough sleep, and she was melting in the heat.

Max went into the room we were going to share and threw his bag on one of the beds. He took out his stuffed penguin and set it on the pillow.

"He needs fresh air," Max said.

He went to the window and pushed open the shutters with a bang.

"Hey, Charlie. That man downstairs who was eating on the car? He's giving some of his food to the cats."

I stuck my head out the window. Now five cats were sitting on the hood of the car. They were all eating rice and beans from the plate, their tails straight up in the air.

"I think we should go for a walk," my father said. "Stretch our legs and see the sights."

My mother yawned. "Maybe that will wake me up."

She went to tell Señora Gloria that we were going out. She was on the balcony with Ledesma. He pointed to the big white palace below.

"Hotel Nacional," he said very proudly. "Beautiful. *Muy bonito*. I take you."

Then I saw it. The purple hairless dog. It was at the far end of the balcony behind a wire fence. It was a small dog, but it probably looked even smaller because it had no hair.

I had never thought about what kind of skin dogs have. And how much smaller they look when they don't have hair, or fur. Especially when they are purple.

But not purple all over. Blotches of purple, as if someone had painted parts of it here and there.

Señora Gloria caught me staring at her dog.

"Elvis tiene una enfermedad," she said, looking very serious, *"de la piel."*

She pulled at the skin of her arm, then put on a sad face.

I got the picture. Elvis the dog had something wrong with its skin, so Señora Gloria shaved it and painted some medicine on it. Purple medicine.

I wondered how the dog felt about the color.

"Poor dog," said Max. "Can we take him for a walk with us?"

"I don't think that's such a great idea," my mother said. "He looks sick."

"It's not his fault he's purple."

Max put one finger through the wire fence. Elvis came over and licked it. His tongue was purple, too.

"When I grow up, I'm going to be a vet," Max announced. "I'll take care of sick dogs and sick birds and sick bugs and —"

Ledesma clapped his hands.

"Animal doctor! Good idea! *Ahora vámonos.* Let's go."

Max looked disappointed as we said goodbye to Señora Gloria and followed Ledesma down the hallway. He punched the elevator button over and over.

I looked through the grill. The elevator was nowhere in sight. There was just a huge, dark, bottomless pit.

"Let's walk," my father suggested. "We could use the exercise."

The stairs were fine with me. That *elevador* gave me the creeps.

Outside, my parents put on their straw hats, which made them look like farmers. I wondered if they did this sort of thing just to embarrass me. We headed toward the Hotel Nacional, right at the foot of our street. The grass was smooth and perfect like a golf course.

When we reached the marble steps that led to the front door of the hotel, Ledesma stopped.

"Adiós," he said. "I go now."

"Ledesma," my mother said, "please come and have a drink with us."

His face looked a little pained. "*Gracias,* Señora, but it is not a place for me. It is a place for *turistas.* I will see you soon."

Then he smiled, turned and walked away.

"That's strange," my father said. "He seemed so proud of the hotel. You would have thought he'd built it himself."

"Did he understand we were inviting him?" my mother wondered.

We walked up the steps into an enormous lobby with a very shiny white marble floor. Chandeliers hung from the golden ceiling. There were huge vases of flowers and tall windows that looked onto the sea. Every few steps, a man or a lady in a uniform wished us *Buenos días.*

I looked back through the open door. I could see Señora Gloria's building at the end of the street, with the paint peeling off the front and the pile of rocks and old car. I felt like a time traveler.

We went through another open door and onto a lawn where chairs and tables were scattered here and there.

"Let's sit down and admire the view," my mother said.

"Are we allowed? We're not staying here," Max

said. "Maybe that's why Ledesma didn't want to come in."

Max is like that, always worried. He takes after my father.

"We're allowed," I told him, "but I'm not sure you are."

"Why not?"

I rolled my eyes. "Because you're too small. Do you see anyone else as small as you?"

A waiter came by and dropped off glasses of mango juice with real pieces of mango and a paper umbrella floating on top. And we didn't even ask for them!

I felt like a movie star. There I was, sitting in front of the sea in a lounge chair with comfy cushions, and waiters in uniforms with gold buttons gliding over the perfect green grass, carrying trays.

Not exactly like life in Montreal, where I have to share a juice box with my little brother and try to choke down my father's spinach and wheat germ smoothies for breakfast.

I looked around and noticed that everyone was a tourist. At least, they looked like tourists. They had guidebooks, cameras and sunhats. And they were speaking in loud English, French and Chinese.

The people who worked in the hotel — the waiters and the people at the reception desk and the ones keeping the floor clean — were all Cuban.

Ledesma said that this place was for tourists only. Did that mean Cubans weren't allowed to stay here? It didn't seem fair.

All of a sudden, I heard a loud wail, and the waiters rushed into the hotel.

I looked around. No Max. Then I saw the waiters and a few guests gathered in a circle, staring at something on the marble floor.

I had a sinking feeling that Max was in the middle of that circle. I have this special alert that goes off when I hear his squeaky, angry voice.

I ran toward the crowd of people and pushed my way into the middle.

There was Max, his face whiter than the marble floor except for the red blood dripping from his nose.

I inspected the crime scene.

Clue #1: Max's running shoes were at the far end of the hall.

Clue #2: Max was wearing his socks.

Clue #3: There was a splotch of blood on the wall.

Conclusion: Max had been sock-skating at full speed on the slippery floor, and he forgot to put on his brakes in time.

How can one little kid get into trouble so fast?

A waiter came up carrying a tray with a napkin and ice for Max's nose. My parents finally showed

up. I explained what had happened, based on my investigation. My mother helped Max stand up, and I went and got his running shoes. My father thanked the waiters. He looked very embarrassed about all the fuss.

"Let's go," he said. "Now."

The waiters from the Hotel Nacional gathered on the wide marble steps and waved as we left the building. We did not even have to pay for the mango juice.

In silence, we walked across the lawn to a low wall, and then down a set of steep stairs toward the ocean. For once, Max was quiet.

We had come to the famous seaside walkway. It was full of people doing all kinds of things. Some were standing on the edge of the wall, fishing with long skinny bamboo poles, and buckets of fish at their feet. Musicians were strumming guitars and blowing trumpets. Men were playing dice games, and kids were flying kites. The wind was blowing hard off the water. It was excellent kite weather. Whenever a wave crashed against the wall, fine drops of water washed our faces.

Everyone I saw looked happy. This was more like it!

THREE
The Shooting Gallery

Whenever I go somewhere new, I always read about it first. That was how I knew that Malecón was the name of the seawall, and that Havana used to be called San Cristóbal de la Habana.

Just then Max started pulling on my sleeve. "Hey, what's that big castle up ahead?"

"It's protecting us from attackers."

Max stared at me. "Is this a dangerous place?"

"It used to be. In the old days, pirates and buccaneers loved to attack the city to get their hands on the gold and silver. After a guy named Jacques de Sores stole everything he could and burned down the city, everyone got fed up. So the people built fortresses and castles to protect the place. And it worked. Do you see any pirates?"

Max thought about it very hard. "No. That's because they all ended up in the movies."

Then he put a hand over his eye and waved his arm in the air. "And they're wearing eyepatches and bandanas, and carrying swords and looking mean."

After the seafront, we headed into the city. Clotheslines and electric wires crisscrossed above streets so narrow you could probably jump from a balcony on one side of the street to one on the other. A few of the buildings looked like they were about to fall down.

Maybe that was why the people were out on the sidewalks. They didn't want their houses falling on their heads.

Some men were sitting at folding tables, playing dominos. I always thought dominos was a game for kids, but here grownups were playing, and they were very serious. They slapped down their pieces on the table, shouting and punching the air with their fists, as if they had just won the Stanley Cup and the World Series at the same time.

Meanwhile, kids were playing marbles in the middle of the street. Dogs slept in patches of sunlight, though I didn't see a single purple one. Above our heads, ladies were leaning over their balconies, watching the action below between sheets flapping

in the wind. They were having shouted conversations with the domino players.

There was a baseball game going on in an empty lot. None of the players had gloves, and the ball was wrapped in layers and layers of tape. I couldn't tell which heaps of stones were the bases, but the players must have known.

At the far end of the lot was an old green container. You know, one of those giant, rusty metal boxes that are stacked on ships and trains to carry stuff in?

The door to the container was open, and there were people inside, all of them men.

And they were shooting rifles! I couldn't see what they were shooting at, so I went to have a closer look.

Someone had taped a target at one end of the container, and in the middle of the bullseye was a balloon.

The rifle shots were pretty loud, so I didn't hear my parents and Max come up behind me. A man standing by the container saw my father and asked him if he wanted to try.

"Only ten pesos. Two shots."

My father smiled. He looked embarrassed. "No, no, *gracias*."

I think he was afraid he would miss the target.

"Can I try?" I asked.

"Of course not!" my mother told me. "This is so dangerous! Right in the middle of the city. What would happen if a bullet went through the wall of the container and..."

A gunshot drowned out her voice. Then a balloon popped. Everyone cheered.

Maybe it was dangerous, but it looked like fun. Anyway, I bet they weren't real bullets.

Right next to the container, a bunch of men were standing around an old car with its hood up. They didn't look worried about getting shot by the guys taking target practice. They were too busy arguing about how to fix the car. I didn't understand what they were saying, but when you see a bunch of people around a car with its hood up, what else would they be talking about?

Besides gunshots, there was music everywhere. Flowing out of the windows, the balconies above, and the occasional car that went by with its radio at full blast. Two men were playing guitars in front of an open door. Next to them, two ladies were dancing together very quietly. I know that sounds strange, but it was hot, and I bet they were dancing slowly and quietly so they would stay cool. They danced very well, even in high heels on the rough, rocky street. They must have been practicing all their lives.

I kept looking down at my feet so I wouldn't

trip over the broken pavement. Or what was left of it, since the concrete was all chopped up.

I wouldn't want to walk down this street in the dark. I thought of those movies on TV where the hero goes into a rough neighborhood, and you just know something bad is going to happen.

But it wasn't that way at all on this street, even if some of the buildings were crumbling, and most of the shop windows were

empty. The people didn't have much money compared to where I lived. But they were pretty relaxed, except when they were shouting from their balconies.

And everyone wished us *Buenas tardes* as we walked by.

I turned around and saw a man talking to my parents in a mishmash of Spanish and English. I could tell by the look on my father's face that he did not understand.

When my father told him we lived in Canada, the man put on an enormous smile.

"I have a cousin in Vancouver! You know him?"

My father tried to explain that we lived on the other side of the country from Vancouver, but the man didn't seem to catch on.

"You hungry? I know a restaurant. Come!"

The man took my father by the arm and started leading him down the street.

We all followed. We had no choice.

Usually my parents love talking to people in new countries. They say it's the best way to get to know a place. Better than reading guidebooks.

But not this time. My father dragged his feet and tried to pull away from the man without being rude.

He looked back at my mother. What was going on?

Both my parents wanted to get away from the man with the cousin in Vancouver.

"Restaurant! This way! Cousin in Vancouver!"

The next minute we were standing in front of a cart loaded with big pots boiling over a gas burner, like those stoves people use for camping. The man gave us another big smile. A woman was standing behind the stove, stirring whatever was in the pots.

I understood. The man didn't really want to be our friend. And I bet he didn't have a cousin in Vancouver, either. He was out scouting for customers. People like us who didn't know how to say No, thanks. Or who were too polite to tell him to go away.

He probably picked us because we looked one hundred percent like foreigners.

My father sniffed at the two banged-up pots on the gas burners. Whatever was cooking smelled really good to me.

Why were my parents scared of eating here? They were always telling us to try new things and to taste something before saying we didn't like it.

"Muy rico," the man said.

My father looked at my mother. They both shook their heads.

"Come on, boys," he said to us. "We'll find somewhere else to eat."

I understood. My father didn't like the way the man had tricked him, acting so friendly when he only wanted to sell us something.

I looked back. The man had a sad expression, and so did his wife. They had just lost their only customers.

If I'd had a choice, which I never do, I would have eaten there. Just one little bowl of something. Those people really seemed to need customers.

We walked back along the Malecón. The sea below was dark blue. The sun was sinking into the

water. When it disappeared without even a splash, some people having a picnic on the seawall burst into applause.

I guess they figured the sun had done a very good job, even if it was the same one every day.

Max looked at the people's picnic. Rice, beans and something that looked like fried bananas.

"I'm hungry," he announced.

If my brother catches just a glimpse of food, his mouth starts to water. Sort of like Pavlov's dog.

It was a good thing the people didn't understand him! They probably would have shared their food with him.

Just before we reached Señora Gloria's apartment, we passed a restaurant called La Roca. A line of people stretched out the front door and down the sidewalk.

"Look at that crowd," my father said. "They must have really good food."

We took our place at the end of the line. But after fifteen minutes of waiting, the line had not moved an inch.

"I don't know about this," my mother said, yawning.

We were the only impatient ones. Everyone else was waiting calmly. A couple of men playing guitars and singing walked up and down the sidewalk, which helped the time go by faster. One of them had a little basket attached to his guitar, and people were dropping in money.

The musicians were really good. Back home they would have been stars.

"Maybe there are so many people," my mother added, "not because it's a good place. Maybe it's the only place."

A woman came out of the restaurant patting her stomach. That was a start, but it would take a lot more people leaving if we were going to eat before midnight.

Then a man walked right up to us.

"Come," he said.

We stared at him. Were we really going to cut in front of all these people? The man was wearing a white shirt with *La Roca* written on it. Maybe it was his restaurant.

We followed the man in the white shirt past the whole line of people. No one said anything or acted mad. It was like we were Very Important Persons. Though I didn't know why.

The inside of the restaurant was as dark as a cave and as cold as the inside of a freezer. Maybe that was why the place was so popular: the air-conditioning.

The man led us to a table, and we sat down.

"Now why did that happen?" my mother wondered.

"It's because we're famous," Max decided.

"Not exactly," my father said. "It's because we're foreigners."

"They must think we're going to spend a lot of money," my mother added.

I was tired and just happy to be sitting down.

A waitress arrived — not with the menu, but with plates of food. Big heaps of rice and beans. Everybody around us was eating the same thing.

How would we spend a lot of money if they brought us the same thing everyone else was eating? That was a mystery without a solution.

Still, I felt embarrassed about cutting in front of all those people. I stopped looking around and decided to eat fast, so we could give our seats to someone in line.

FOUR
School Days

The next morning, Max and I were having breakfast — another huge plate of rice and beans. Max was slipping beans one by one to Elvis, under the table.

All of a sudden, the front door flew open, and a woman thumped into the apartment. Elvis barked excitedly, ran down the hall and sniffed her running shoes like they were doggy treats.

The woman and Señora Gloria gave each other a giant hug.

"This is my friend Mercedes," Señora Gloria said. "She will be taking you to the school. She works there."

Did I tell you? We would be going to school during our vacation. My mother, you see, writes picture books for little kids. She thought it would be a good idea if we spent part of our winter break in a school in Havana, talking to kids about reading, writing stories and drawing. We would get to know the country in a different way than everyone else, she promised.

Maybe later we would get to have our own vacation. With my parents, you never know.

Mercedes immediately started talking like a house on fire. A great storm of Spanish words. My mother's eyes grew wider and wider. I don't think she caught half of what Mercedes was saying. I know I didn't.

But I did figure out that Mercedes was explaining where we were going, and how, and who we would be meeting. She seemed to be saying how difficult the students were, how they didn't listen, how they had no discipline. She waved her hands in the air to show how wild they were.

She ended her speech by asking my mother, *"Tu español es muy bueno, verdad?"* Your Spanish is very good, right?

My mother cleared her throat. *"Sí,"* she said in a small voice.

Mercedes looked at her watch.

"Vámonos," she yelled, and headed for the door.

I think she was the only person in Havana who was in a hurry.

On the way out, my mother grabbed her big portfolio full of books and paper and markers and pencils.

Mercedes did not like the *elevador* any more than we did. She flew down the stairs like a raging bull was chasing her. My rice and beans bounced around in my stomach as I followed.

A minute later, we were standing on the Malecón.

"Taxi!" she shouted, waving her arms in the air like a windmill.

A second later, a swarm of motorbikes appeared, buzzing like bees.

Mercedes jumped onto the nearest one and grabbed the driver's belt.

"I don't know about this," my mother said. "It looks dangerous. The driver isn't even wearing a helmet."

She was right. I could just imagine her hanging onto the motorbike driver with one hand and holding her portfolio in the other as it flapped in the wind like a sail.

Just in time, help arrived! A motorbike zoomed up that had a trailer attached to it, with two facing benches and an awning on top.

We climbed on and followed Mercedes down the street, past palm trees and buildings of all different colors. They looked like a line of sherbet tubs in an ice cream shop: pistachio green, lemon yellow, pink grapefruit... though I don't know if anyone makes sherbet out of grapefruit.

Our taxi stopped on a square, next to Mercedes. The buildings were decorated with columns and domes and stone curlicues. Some of the domes were covered in gold.

"Plaza Vieja," our driver said.

The square lived up to its name. It was very old,

with a fountain in the middle. First thing in the morning, and a band was already playing music by the splashing fountain, and people were dancing in a lazy kind of way.

We climbed down from the trailer, and a couple took our place — an old woman wearing a long white wedding dress, and an old man in a straw hat, smoking a cigar.

We went down a little street to a tall stone doorway that looked like the entrance to a castle.

Was this a school? We walked into a garden filled with flowers and more palm trees. Birds were singing loudly, as if they were having a contest. Watched over by two teachers, a dozen or so schoolkids were sitting at a long table beneath the trees, waiting for us.

Imagine having school outside, in the middle of winter!

As we walked over to the table, the kids stood up all at once and said, *"Buenos días, Señora."*

For a moment, my mother got that deer-in-the-headlights look.

Then she had a great idea. She told the kids that she did not speak Spanish very well, and that they would have to help her out.

Not just a great idea. A genius idea. The kids I know love to correct their teachers, and their parents, too.

My mother read one of her books in Spanish. Another good move. She didn't have to make up the words. They were already there on the page.

Then she had a third good idea. A picture is worth a thousand words, everyone knows. She got out long rolls of paper she had brought in her portfolio and covered the table with them like a tablecloth. Then she set out felt-tip markers and asked the kids to draw a picture of their families.

Mercedes seemed to say that the kids were difficult and had no discipline. It didn't look that way to me. They did not touch the markers until my mother told them they could. And when they started drawing, they used only a tiny corner of the paper in front of them.

Maybe they were afraid of taking up too much room or wasting paper. Maybe they didn't have many school supplies. I didn't see any pencil boxes or books on the table.

Some of them had pretty unusual families. One girl drew nothing but birdcages with birds inside.

The boy next to her drew a big boat of a car like the ones we saw on the street. Another boy drew a picture of himself as tall as a giant, and everyone else in his family came up to his knees.

My mother moved along the rows of kids, telling them that their pictures were great. *"Más grande,"* she told them, trying to get the kids to use all the paper.

Meanwhile, Mercedes and the teachers looked worried. They might have thought the kids were wasting the art supplies or making a mess. Or drawing something that wasn't true, because in real life, who had a family of birdcages?

Max grabbed a marker from the table. I just knew he wanted to do a portrait of our family. Luckily, my father made him put the marker back and decided it was time for the two of them to go exploring. The next minute, they went out the door. I was happy to stay.

Most of the kids stuck to their little section of the paper. Then all that changed. The boy who drew himself as a giant stood up, pushed his bench closer to the table and kneeled on it. He started drawing a giant portrait of himself — or maybe it was a monster from outer space — that went halfway across the paper.

When the other kids saw what he was doing, they picked up their markers. Pretty soon the long roll of paper was an explosion of color and shapes and strange families — some of them inside their houses, or on motorbikes, or flying over the sea. The teachers couldn't believe what was happening.

In my school, the kids would be pushing and shoving and making fun of each other's drawings or fighting over the markers. Here, the older ones helped the younger ones who were just learning how to draw.

By the end of the morning, we had an enormous family portrait on several rolls of paper. I helped my mother tape the sheets to one of the stone walls in the garden, since we would be coming back the next day.

It was time for lunch. The kids lined up by the door, very straight and very quiet. Their teachers gave the signal, and they all filed out of the garden and into the street.

"Hasta mañana," Mercedes called.

All of a sudden, everything was silent. I could hear the birds singing in the trees. I felt exhausted, as if I had run around the block ten times.

My mother wiped the sweat off her forehead. Teaching is hard work! But maybe I'd try it myself some day.

"Well, that could have been worse," my mother said as we walked back up the street toward the Plaza Vieja.

"You were great," I told her.

"Pretty good for Day One," she admitted.

We met up with my father and Max on the square. They'd found a little restaurant with tables under the palm trees. Palm trees are pretty skinny, and they don't give much shade. We had to keep moving our chairs around so we wouldn't get fried by the sun.

And, of course, there was a band: three trumpet players in white suits. In this place, you didn't need an iPod for music.

At the table next to us, a bunch of old guys with mustaches like Ledesma's were arguing away at the top of their lungs.

Were they going to start fighting? Did hundred-year-old men fight in Cuba?

The waiter came by. He looked at the old men, then at us.

"Esquina caliente," he said, pointing his chin in their direction. "Baseball."

I got it! The *esquina caliente* was the hot corner. Back home we called it the hot stove league — a bunch of old guys arguing about last night's games in the middle of winter.

— • —

For the next two days, we met with the kids and their teachers in the school in the garden. On the third day, the last one, the big rolls of paper were hanging on the wall where we'd left them, and all the kids were waiting at the table very quietly. Blackbirds were whistling in the trees above the teachers' heads. It sounded to me like the birds were making fun of the teachers for thinking that their students were difficult.

The kids looked happy when my mother and I walked in. Our visit was a break for them.

Each day, my mother was less nervous than the day before. And Mercedes relaxed a little, too. So did I.

My mother knew exactly what she was going to tell the kids, since she had rehearsed with me on the balcony. She wanted them to write a little story about their families based on the pictures they had drawn.

I wondered what the girl with the birdcages would write, or the boy who was a giant compared to everyone else in his house.

One of the teachers came up to my mother with a worried look.

"Algunos niños no saben escribir." Some of the children, she warned, didn't know how to write.

My mother kept her cool. She said to the group, "If you need help with writing, you can ask me, or a friend, or my son Charlie."

Me? How could I help them when they were writing in Spanish?

Right away, the girl with the birdcage family came over to me.

"Puedes ayudarme?"

How could I say no? Pretty soon, the kids were talking about their stories with each other and writing everything down. Even the teachers jumped in. They were surprised that the younger students could write stories. The teachers were learning at the same time as the kids.

Finally, our work day was over. I was ready to stop being a teacher. I was tired from all the kids wanting me to read their stories and tell them what I thought, in a language I half-spoke. The blackbirds kept dropping out of the trees and landing on the table trying to eat the kids' fruit snacks, and I had to chase them away. It was a big job!

At the very end, my mother took a photo with the kids in front of the big picture they had drawn the first day. She asked them to hold up their stories, and they waved them in the air.

The teachers wanted to be in the photo, too. They looked very proud. Mercedes must have changed her mind about how difficult the students were.

When my mother announced she was leaving the art supplies and a bunch of her books for the kids, they all cheered.

One of the teachers looked like a movie star

with long black curly hair, red lips and giant silver earrings. She herded the kids into a line and they all paraded past my mother to thank her and give her a kiss on the cheek.

I stayed away from that line.

Then we all shook hands with the teachers, *con mucho gusto* and *mucho placer*. Before I knew it, the movie star teacher kissed me on the cheek. I didn't have a choice.

The kids left in single file as the blackbirds whistled goodbye.

School was over. Now the real vacation could begin!

FIVE
The Magic Street

After our school days, my parents wanted to relax. I tried to be quiet, too. I sat on the balcony and looked at the water as my father read and my mother sketched the view. Max was busy explaining to Elvis why he had purple spots.

"Don't feel bad," he told the dog. "They look like grape popsicles."

Pretty soon my father fell asleep with his face in his book. And I knew better than to disturb my mother when she was drawing.

This was getting pretty boring. I didn't want to waste my time on the balcony. I wanted to explore the city.

The first time I saw Señora Gloria's building, I could not believe I was actually going to live here. And I admit, I was a little afraid.

But not anymore. The city was full of friendly people.

"I'm going to go for a walk," I whispered to my parents. I didn't want Max to hear.

My father was asleep. My mother was in her own world. And Max was with his best friend.

I headed for the door and ran down the stairs. I figured if I got lost, I would just ask someone where the Hotel Nacional was. From there, it was easy.

I walked toward the center of the city, toward the school, the castles and the Plaza Vieja. Motorbike taxis swooped past me like bats, offering a ride. But I wanted to walk, and besides, I didn't really know where I was going.

After a while, the buildings started looking a little tired, and the streets filled up with domino players sitting outside around card tables, and all the empty lots had baseball games going on. The guitar players on the sidewalk glanced at me as I went past.

There were plenty of kids my age walking around alone. They must have been running errands or doing odd jobs. I was the only foreigner.

I stopped to watch a baseball game in an empty lot. The guys playing were much older than me, so

I didn't think they would let me be on their team. When one of them made a diving catch with his bare hands, I cheered so they would notice me. But they didn't ask me to play, so I kept walking.

That turned out to be a good thing. At the next corner, I came across a place I never would have seen if I'd joined the game.

Bienvenido al Callejón de Hamel, a big banner over the street read. *Entrada Libre.*

I could get in for free. Which was lucky, since I only had a little change in my pocket.

As soon as I passed under the huge sculpted red arch that had human figures on top and horseshoes for good luck, a small man in a straw hat offered to be my guide.

"Only twenty pesos," he said.

When I said No, thank you, another man dressed all in white made the same offer.

"The best guide in Callejón de Hamel, only fifteen pesos."

I didn't even have that much. I felt uncomfortable. If these men were asking for money from a kid, they must have really needed it. Did they think I was richer than they were?

It was the strangest street I had ever seen. From the pavement to the rooftops, every inch of the walls and windows was painted in bright colorful designs: giant tattooed faces, weird creatures that looked like satellites, poems illustrated with paintings of enormous flowers and magical landscapes. Some of them reminded me of Picasso paintings, or that artist who paints the melting watches.

Not to mention the sculptures made out of old bathtubs, bicycle wheels, upside-down chairs, all painted red and gold and lime green. It was like being part of a painting, or inside an artist's mind. Music was coming out of small booths that lined the street, and when I walked past, the songs changed with every booth. It was like twisting the dial of an old radio.

A woman came up to me. At first I was worried she was another guide. Then she took my hand. She was wearing blue flowers in her hair, giant, clanking silver earrings, and dozens of bracelets and necklaces. Her fingernails were long and green, and she had rings on every finger.

She led me to a little table covered with cards with strange pictures on them.

"I am the fortune-teller of Callejón de Hamel," she said. "I see all and tell all."

I didn't know what to say. I wasn't so sure I wanted to know what was going to happen in the future. What if I didn't like it? And besides, I sort of like surprises.

Anyway, I figured I knew what my future held. Any minute now, a bunch of guitar players would start playing, and people would dance.

"Ah, you do not believe me," the woman went on. She had a gold tooth. "I will tell you something about yourself. And you will understand that I truly see all and tell all."

She stared at my hand, then looked into my eyes.

"You live in Canada," she declared.

"How did you know that?"

The woman laughed loudly. Her gold tooth flashed.

"If you were from the United States, you would not be here. People from the United States cannot come here because of politics."

"Why not?"

"The United States didn't like our revolution. They built a wall around us so nothing could come in from their country." She smiled. "An invisible wall, of course."

"I've seen loads of tourists here," I told her, "at the Hotel Nacional."

"Of course. They are from every country but the United States. Is that where you are staying?"

"No. We're staying with Señora Gloria."

"I see."

Then she took my hand again and ran one long green fingernail along a line in my palm. It tickled.

"You will soon meet someone very close to you."

"That makes no sense," I said to the woman. "I don't know anyone here."

"The ways of fortune are mysterious," she whispered in a dramatic voice. She looked past me.

I turned around.

There was Max, wearing his Max face, sitting in a bathtub sculpture, waving his hands in the air.

"Now you know," the fortune-teller smiled. "I truly do see all."

"Hey, Charlie," Max called. "Come on in, the water's great!"

I couldn't believe my eyes!

"How did you get here, you little spy? And where are Mom and Dad?"

"Back home, snoring on the balcony. It was easy. I followed you," Max said. "I'm good at following people. I could be a great detective."

My parents would be worried, and mad, if they found out that Max had been wandering around Havana alone.

"You're way too young to be walking alone in a big city."

"I wasn't alone. I was right behind you. I knew you would save me if I got attacked by a robber or something."

It was no easier to slip away from my little brother than it was to get rid of my own shadow.

"You do not have to pay," the fortune-teller smiled at me. "But from now on, you must listen to what we fortune-tellers say."

Max jumped out of the bathtub and came over.

"Sorry," he said, but I knew he wasn't really. "I didn't want to sit around the house with Mom and Dad."

I couldn't blame him. "Well, next time, tell me you're following so I can keep an eye on you."

"This place is really cool," he said. "How did you know it was here?"

"The ways of fortune are mysterious," I told him.

"What does that mean?"

"You're too young to understand."

Max stuck out his lower lip. He hates it when I say that.

We went past another little booth. On top of the beaded curtain that hung over the doorway was a sign that said *La Mano Mágica*.

"Come here, Max. You'll like this."

He stuck his nose in.

"No way. I'm not going in there!"

It was a small, dark shop that smelled of dry leaves and dusty animal fur. Bunches of herbs, dried flowers and feathers hung from the ceiling. On the shelves were all sorts of different-shaped bottles filled with colored powders and potions. The burning candles and incense started to give me a headache.

The strangest part were the dolls. Little dolls made of cloth and wood and metal. Some had glass eyes that stared at me.

The woman behind the counter was wearing a long white robe. She was sewing an eye on a doll. She looked up.

"If you have a problem," she said, "I have the answer."

Everyone played at being mysterious here.

The woman held up the doll she was working on. It had hair all over its body, like a one-eyed miniature monkey.

"Muy bonita," I said to her. "Very nice."

With all those dolls in her shop, I didn't want to get on her bad side. Once I saw a scary movie where a doll comes to life and does bad things. I wanted to make sure that didn't happen here.

Callejón de Hamel was like a fair for magicians and people who cast spells for a living. Every little booth had something new and strange to sell.

In one booth, a man was standing by a camping stove, cooking up a big pot of some kind of green juice the color of frogs that had been put through a blender.

I knew I had to take Max back home to our parents. But there were so many things to see here.

"Hey, Max, I'll buy you a glass," I offered. "Don't you want to turn into a frog?"

"Stop that!"

I thought I was making a joke, but Max was really upset. His bottom lip was trembling. I had gone a little too far.

"Don't worry, Max. I'm not going to turn you into a frog. Mom and Dad might get mad at me."

He looked relieved.

We came to the end of the street. A man was standing on an upside-down bathtub reciting poetry while two men behind him played guitars, just like in my prediction for the future.

Who needed a fortune-teller?

Max and I listened for a while, even if we couldn't

understand everything the poet was saying. Something about *amor* and *lágrimas*, love and tears. But we could understand the guitars perfectly.

When the man finished his poem, we applauded along with everyone else. I put the few coins I had into the tin can he passed around.

I looked up and down the street, at the paintings on the wall and the sculptures made of junk. I had a strange thought. All the art, the murals and the sculptures and everything else reminded me of the drawings the kids had done at the school.

Everyone was a musician here, and everyone was an artist. Even the schoolkids.

Max and I began walking through the labyrinth of streets, heading back to the Hotel Nacional. At least, I hoped we were going in that direction. A labyrinth is like a maze. Once you go in, there's no telling when you'll get out.

It was starting to get dark, and I wasn't too sure of the way. I wondered what my parents would say. They wanted to have adventures, but that didn't mean they wanted Max and me to get lost in Havana.

I decided to take a shortcut through a huge vacant lot scattered with piles of rubble.

All of a sudden, I heard wild barking, and a pack of scruffy, drooling dogs ran toward us.

Max froze. I couldn't blame him.

But the dogs paid no attention to us. They must have been on their way to a dog restaurant somewhere. At least I hoped so. They were so skinny I could see their ribs.

"Where are their houses?" Max asked once they had gone.

"They live in the streets," I told him. "Maybe their owners abandoned them, or maybe they never had houses. Now they run in packs, looking for food and a place to sleep."

Max shook his head. "Poor dogs. We should adopt one and take him back home with us."

"I bet Miro would love to share his house with a dog that would probably swallow him whole."

Miro is our cat, who is convinced he is the king of our house.

Suddenly, the pack of snarling dogs did a U-turn and ran straight at us.

I shoved Max behind me. "Don't move!" I ordered.

At the last moment, the dogs swerved around us. For a second or two we stood in a swirling mass of dark fur and sharp teeth. Then they disappeared through a hole in a fence.

Max's face was white as a ghost. Mine must have been, too.

"Don't tell Mom and Dad about the dogs," I said to him.

"Don't worry."

"And nothing about that street, either."

"I promise," Max agreed.

We finally did find our way back to Señora Gloria's building. Our parents were still sitting on the balcony like a couple of statues.

That night I dreamed I had cured the purple dog with a magic doll that did only good things.

SIX
Apple's House

Finally, it was time to say goodbye to Señora Gloria and her purple dog. Max kneeled down in front of Elvis and, believe it or not, hugged him — even his ugly purple patches.

"I'll miss you," he told the dog, "but we'll be back."

Elvis wagged his tail and barked, and Señora Gloria smiled.

We were leaving Havana to explore some of the rest of the island. Our vacation could begin. It was about time.

"We're going to a place called Viñales," my father told us. "It's world-famous for its mogotes."

"What's that?" Max wanted to know.

"You'll see," my father promised.

My mother was more helpful.

"They're little green mountains," she said. "From far away, they look enormous. But when you come closer, you see they're really very small. That's called an optical illusion."

I could see the little wheels turning in Max's head as he thought about this.

We learned about optical illusions in school. The animal in one drawing looked like a duck and a rabbit at the same time. It all depended on how you looked at it.

Meanwhile, we walked past the wrecked car with cats sleeping on it, and down to the parking lot of the Hotel Nacional. That was where we would catch the bus.

The only people waiting for the bus were foreigners. There wasn't a single Cuban in the line. Everyone had guidebooks and hi-tech water bottles and binoculars to watch birds.

"It's a tourist bus, I guess," my mother said.

"Cubans and foreigners can't ride on the same buses," my father added. "Those are government rules."

First the hotel, and now the bus! I wondered why the government wanted to separate us from Cubans. Maybe they didn't want us to talk to each other. But why not?

It was strange, because I had met dozens of kids, kissed a teacher who looked like a movie star and stayed in Señora Gloria's house.

That didn't make sense. There were all these rules, but only part of the time.

We started out on the longest, dustiest trip I had ever been on, even if Viñales was not that far, at least not on the map. I wanted to look out the window, but the bus was so hot I kept falling asleep.

I woke up once and saw crowds of people on bicycles pedaling down the highway. I fell asleep again, and the next time I opened my eyes, the bus was passing a horse pulling a cart heaped high with palm tree branches with wide green leaves. I fell asleep one more time, and the bus driver woke me up with his singing. In the middle of a field stood a single lonely tree with bark like elephant skin.

Finally, we pulled up next to a tall wooden barn on a farm where crops were growing. I followed everyone out of the bus and into the barn.

It wasn't a barn with animals. Inside, ladies were rolling cigars. It looked like they were making Plasticine snakes, the way I used to do when I was a kid.

The ladies turned to stare at us, then went back to their work. High above their heads, in the rafters, wide tobacco leaves were drying in the heat and dust.

It felt a little strange. These people were work-

ing, and we showed up in a bus to watch them as if we were at a museum. No one would do that where I lived. Besides, smoking is bad for you, so why were we at a cigar factory?

After a few minutes we went back outside, and most of the passengers stopped to buy boxes of cigars from a counter next to the barn.

My father told us that Cuban cigars were the best in the world.

"How do you know? You don't even smoke," I said.

"Everyone knows that. That's why people come all the way here to buy them."

I could think of better things to do than shop for cigars.

A little later, we stopped in front of a cliff. There were two enormous murals painted on the bare rock. One showed prehistoric animals that must have lived here a long time ago. And the other was a picture of crowds of people cheering a giant Che Guevara.

He really got around, and everyone seemed to love him. Even the tourists. A man took out his guidebook and started reading aloud.

"According to the stories, Che met Fidel Castro in Mexico, and together they plotted to overthrow the dictator Batista. They invaded Cuba in 1956, and finally took power in 1959. Che was the primary advisor to Castro's government. He was also the director of an infamous prison."

He couldn't have been one hundred percent a good guy.

We climbed back onto the bus, and I fell asleep a minute later. When I opened my eyes, we were pulling onto the main street of Viñales in a great cloud of dust.

The town looked like it belonged in a cowboy movie. A single red dirt street with more horses than cars, and low wood buildings on both sides, and people leaning in the doorways, watching us. Some of the buildings had those swinging wooden half-doors, just like in the movies. I wondered if a gunfight would break out between the sheriff and the bad guys.

And sure enough, there were mogotes.

My mother was right. A mogote was a little hump of a mountain covered in trees, set in the middle of the fields. Like a mini mountain that had fallen out of the sky and landed here.

We walked out of the cloud of dust and went in search of the house my parents had rented for the next few days. Finding it was not going to be easy. In Viñales, there were no street names.

Everyone was very polite. They gave us directions to the house, even if they didn't know where it was and had never heard of it.

Before long we were lost. But not too lost, since the town had only one street.

We finally found the place on a dirt track behind the main street, just as the wheels were about to fall off my mother's rolling suitcase.

"What a beautiful garden!" she said.

It was her kind of spot, with millions of flowering trees, which meant there were ten million butterflies and birds. Even my father had to admit it was pretty.

There was only one problem. I knew what it was by the way the owner came walking toward us after carefully closing the gate behind her. With every step she took, a little cloud of red dust rose up at her feet.

There was no room for us, the woman told us. Her house was full. It was all a mistake.

She didn't even try to look sorry.

"Señora Gloria called you and reserved," my mother said.

The woman shrugged her shoulders as if it wasn't her fault. Then she waved goodbye and went back into her pretty garden, closing the gate carefully.

My mother and my father stared at each other. They were in a state of shock.

Here we were, in the middle of nowhere, not knowing anyone, and we had no place to stay.

And the sun would be going down soon.

Even Max knew better than to say anything.

"I can't believe this," my mother said. She looked back at the pretty garden with the butterflies and the birds. I had never seen her so sad.

In the silence, I heard a *clip-clop*. A big horse was coming slowly down the road in our direction. A barefoot boy a little older than me was riding him, without a saddle. I wondered how he managed not to fall off.

He stopped in front of us. He looked at us standing there with our bags in front of the closed garden gate.

"Hotel problem?" he said shyly and pointed at the house.

My mother put on a sad face. That wasn't very hard.

The boy smiled.

"La casa de Manzana," he said. "That's what you need. She's my aunt."

We followed him as he clip-clopped slowly down the dusty red road. We must have been quite a sight — a family of four with all their luggage walking through the countryside behind a barefoot boy on a horse.

Every now and again he turned around to make sure we hadn't disappeared.

Where would we have gone? There was nothing but fields on all sides, and cows with long curly horns. A skinny white bird was perched on the back of every cow, as if it was waiting for the cow to get a move on.

The birds were there to eat the flies that bothered the cows. It was a good deal for both animals. The birds got lunch, and the cows could relax because they weren't getting bitten.

We walked through clouds of butterflies that got caught in my mother's hair.

"See?" my father said. "That house back there isn't the only one with butterflies."

He was trying to cheer her up. She smiled just a little.

A flock of girls ran past us, laughing like they were heading off to a big party. They were wearing long red and blue dresses that dragged in the dust, and they were decorated with feathers and spangles. As they ran, they fanned themselves with little paper fans.

The boy on the horse watched them hurry by.

"Las bailarinas," the boy said.

Sitting on his horse, he imitated someone dancing.

One thing I've learned about traveling. A lot of the time things don't turn out the way they are supposed to. But if you're lucky, sometimes they turn out better.

The boy jumped down from his horse, reached into the sack slung over his shoulder and took out a carrot. As the horse chewed very noisily and slurped down bits of carrot, the boy pointed to a tiny house with an even smaller porch and a thatched roof.

"La casita de Manzana," he announced proudly.

A woman stepped out. She was so small, it looked like she was made for the cabin. She waved and smiled.

Would we be sharing the casita with her? We would never all fit into that cabin.

"Soy Manzana," she said, pointing to herself.

I had never met anyone named Apple before. Maybe she got the name because she had a perfectly round face.

My mother went to shake her hand, but she hugged my mother instead. My mother hugged her back, even though they had known each other for about two seconds.

Maybe that was the way people said hello to total strangers in Viñales.

Manzana led us into the house. It turned out there was a second house hidden behind a gigantic mass of flowers where she lived. We wouldn't be sharing our place with a stranger named Apple after all. That was a relief!

When my mother discovered the house hidden

behind the flowers, I knew what she would say. And she said it.

"What a beautiful place! And the view of the mogotes! We're lucky after all! And look at those clematis bushes," she went on. "They're enormous!"

In case you don't know, clematis is a flower. A purple one. Just the kind my mother likes.

Both my parents were smiling now. The house was what they called "authentic." The roof was made of dried palm-tree branches, the kind I saw from the bus. They were a little bit like straw. If the Big Bad Wolf ever came by, we would be in trouble.

At least the rest of the house was made of wood. A covered porch faced straight onto the famous mogotes, which you could see if you pushed the flowers out of the way.

We thanked the boy on the horse for helping us and took our bags inside.

"See you again," he called as he rode away.

As we were unpacking, with Manzana looking on and Max searching for the perfect place for his stuffed penguin, a man with a thick mustache came through the open door carrying a television, followed by a boy holding one of those old rabbit-ear antennas.

The boy set up the antenna while the man plugged in the TV.

"No, no," my father said, waving his finger.

Manzana and her family stared at him. Who would say no to a television?

"We don't watch," my father said to Manzana and her family.

"Yes, we do!" Max cried.

My mother tried to repeat the message in Spanish. Manzana, her husband and her son stared at her. They must have thought we were crazy for refusing a television.

Manzana's husband shrugged and picked up the set and walked out the door followed by his family, as Max watched sadly.

"It's okay," I told Max. "You wouldn't have understood the programs anyway."

"Some people have learned a new language by watching TV," my father pointed out.

I wonder about my father sometimes. First he turns down the television. Then he says how useful it could have been.

"Why would the family give up their TV for us?" he went on. "We have television back home. We're here to do something different."

I turned to Max.

"Come on," I said to cheer him up. "Let's go exploring."

We did not have to go far. We went out the door, turned right and found ourselves in the combination living room, dining room and kitchen — all of it outside. There was a table with a spotted dog sleeping under it, surrounded by chickens on the lookout for bugs to eat.

Max immediately crawled under the table to pet the dog. Another small, ugly dog. At least it had hair.

A sink for doing the dishes stood on one side, and next to it was a washing machine. Right above our heads, laundry was flapping on a clothesline propped up by poles.

It was like being in a house, but without the walls. Though there was a roof. A piece of canvas sheltered us from the sun.

Three small cabins the size of our casita were set around the outdoor room. Manzana stepped out of one of them, followed by the man with the mustache. They were carrying plates of fruit. Manzana ran through all the names in Spanish as if she were a teacher: *piña, papaya, naranja, guayaba…*

Then she pointed to the dog busy licking Max's face. Ick! How could he stand it?

"This is Monty. *Y mi marido, Alfredo,*" she added.

She named the fruit and the dog before she introduced her husband.

The next minute my parents came in. Well, not exactly "in" because we were outside, but you get the picture.

My mother thought this was the most beautiful fruit plate she had ever seen. I wasn't so sure. There were pumpkin-colored pieces with green skin and black seeds. And something that looked like a lime on the outside, but with pink flesh like a grapefruit.

"I wonder if they taste as weird as they look," Max whispered.

"There's only one way to find out," I told him, picking up a piece of something sweet and juicy and strange.

Once Max and I were full of fruit, we left our parents to finish their coffee and went down a road that wound between the red and green fields where tobacco was growing. We came across one of those trees with the elephant skin that I had seen from the bus. It was growing all by itself, the only one of its kind in a field as red as a brick.

I went closer and saw it was covered with thorns. No wonder it was all alone.

We walked farther into the fields with ugly birds circling above us. They were bald, and their necks were red, as if they had been dipped in blood. And they were calling out angrily.

"Those are vultures," I told Max. "They like to eat dead things."

"I'm not dead," Max answered.

"Maybe they know something you don't," I said. "Sooner or later, everyone dies, you know."

"Stop that, Charlie!" Max yelled.

Time for some fascinating facts about vultures.

"You know, Max, if a vulture eats too much and gets too heavy to fly, it just throws up until it's light enough to get back into the air again. Cool, huh?"

For some reason, Max didn't appreciate my science lesson.

"We're not dead," Max shouted at the birds, waving his arms like a windmill.

The vultures went on crying in voices that sounded like creaking prison doors.

A flock of hummingbirds flew right past our heads. They darted past at top speed, inches from our ears, and all I could see were flashes of shiny purple and green feathers. They were in a big hurry to visit the next flower.

If you were a hummingbird, Viñales was the place to be. There were flowers everywhere, as big as dinner plates and bright red and pink, so the hummingbirds would be sure to notice them.

The strangest flower belonged to the banana tree.

Everyone knows that bananas come from the store. But before that, they come from trees.

They look like palm trees, with the bananas growing on a top branch. An enormous bright purple ball was hanging at the end of the branch in front of us. That was the banana flower.

I heard laughing and turned around. A whole family on horseback had stopped, and they were pointing at us. The father was wearing a straw hat, and he had a machete hanging from his belt. He was riding an enormous brown horse, and two giggling girls were sitting on the horse in front of him.

On another horse were two barefoot boys, who probably thought it was the funniest thing in the world to be staring at a banana tree the way we were. Here they grew everywhere, like pine trees in our country.

"Jorge!" the man called. *"Sube por favór!"*

He pointed to the tree. One of the boys Max's age had a machete in his belt — just like his father's, but smaller. He jumped down from his horse and scrambled up the tree using his hands and feet. He hacked off a bunch of ripe bananas, shinnied back down the trunk and handed them to me. Then he climbed back on his horse.

Just before the family rode off, the man tipped his hat to us, and we thanked him for the present as the kids waved.

I wondered what it would be like to travel that way, instead of taking the bus or the subway or the car. To go to school, I'd just hop on my horse and gallop across the dusty red fields. And pick some fresh bananas on the way.

SEVEN
The Hollow Mountain

The roosters woke me up at dawn. A loud chorus of them, accompanied by a gang of barking dogs, including Monty.

The Viñales alarm clock! I couldn't believe my parents and Max were still snoring away. This was my chance!

A family vacation can be fun. But sometimes I just had to get away from them. We were together *all* the time. I wanted to go off on my own without Max. If that was possible.

I dressed quickly and tiptoed out of the cabin. I ran down the dirt road and turned around once, then twice.

No Max. It was my lucky day!

The sun was coming up over the fields. Along with the roosters and dogs, clouds of black whistling crows flew in low circles over the ground. A man was plowing his land with the help of two white water buffalo.

The road dipped down toward a pond, and I saw the boy who had guided us to Manzana's house. He was sitting on a rickety pier washing his horse in a pond.

Actually, the horse was washing himself, kneeling down so that only his head stuck out of the water, then bobbing up again and shaking himself off. The boy was keeping an eye on him, holding on to his rope and talking to him.

I was surprised, but it did make sense. People wash their cars where I live, so why wouldn't they wash their horses here?

The boy looked up and saw me and waved.

"Welcome to the Viñales horse wash," he called. "Do you have a horse you want to wash?" He laughed. "Delfín loves it."

I took a few steps down toward the pond.

"He must get pretty dusty."

The boy stood up. "I wash him every day. I think he's clean now."

He pulled on the rope gently, talking to his horse in Spanish.

As soon as the horse was out of the pond, he shook himself again, very hard, and water flew everywhere.

Now we were the ones who needed washing.

"Lázaro," he said, and held out his hand.

"Charlie."

He patted the horse.

"He's Delfín. Where are you going?"

"To the ballfield. I went by it when we arrived here but I didn't have time to stop."

Lázaro got this uncomfortable look.

"It's too early for a game," he told me. "But even if there was one, they probably wouldn't let you play. You have to be signed up on an official team. The rules, you know."

"There sure are a lot of rules here."

"You said it! Most of the time I live in Miami. Not so many rules."

Ah-ha! That was why he spoke such good English. We walked with Delfín onto the dusty road.

"Have you seen the mogotes yet?"

"It's hard not to," I said.

"I mean, from close up?"

"Not yet."

Lázaro took hold of Delfín's mane, and with one leg, he vaulted up onto the horse's back.

"Now do what I did. You're strong enough."

It was easier said than done. After a couple

tries, and with Lázaro's help, there I was, all of a sudden, sitting behind my new friend on Delfín's back. With a horse's eye view of the fields and the mogotes in the distance.

"Hold on to me," Lázaro told me. I grabbed his shoulders and tightened my legs around Delfín's middle. Lázaro didn't gallop too fast, but still, we kicked up clouds of red dust, and birds went shooting up into the air as we went by.

I'd never ridden a horse before. It was a little scary, and pretty bumpy, but it was great!

"I live in Miami with my mother," Lázaro shouted over his shoulder. "But whenever there's a break, I come to see my father's family. People always ask me which place I like best. That's the wrong question. I like both places. I wouldn't want to have to choose."

"Even with all the rules here?"

"Even with all the rules." He laughed. "Hey, I bet you're Canadian."

"You won't believe it, but the last person who told me that was a fortune-teller in Havana," I said.

"I don't need a crystal ball to know. We don't see very many Americans in Cuba. And even fewer in Viñales."

"But you're American. Or at least half-American."

"And half-Cuban. Lots of people think Americans can't come here, but every day planes fly from Miami to Havana. I know, I take them all the time."

"That doesn't make sense," I told him.

He shrugged. "There may be a lot of rules here. But there's always a way around them."

We reached the first mogote. It wasn't so big after all. It just looked tall compared to the flat fields. My mother was right about optical illusions.

Lázaro jumped down from Delfín and helped me slide off the horse. It was easier getting off than getting on. Lázaro thanked him for the ride with a carrot.

"These things are famous." He slapped the side of the mountain. "People come from all over the world to see them. I don't know why."

"My guidebook said there are no rock formations exactly like these anywhere in the world."

"They write about mogotes in guidebooks? You must be kidding," he laughed.

Maybe when you see something every day, I thought, it becomes ordinary.

We walked along the edge of the little mountain that was covered in trees and vines.

Then, through a tangle of plants, I spotted an old rusty metal door on the side of the mountain.

"Look at that!" I said. "Where do you think it goes?"

"I don't know. But I do know we're not supposed to go in."

"Another rule."

"For sure. A serious one."

We looked at each other, then burst out laughing.

All of a sudden, just like that, we knew what we wanted to do.

A rock was pushed up against the metal door to keep it shut. I rolled it away. Lázaro pulled on the handle. It was rusty and wouldn't move.

"I don't think anyone has opened this for years," I said.

"They obey the rules."

The two of us got together and yanked on the handle.

"Uno, dos, tres!" Lázaro shouted.

The door flew open and we ended up on our behinds on the ground. We picked ourselves up and went back to the door, then stuck our heads into the opening.

The air was damp and cool and smelled of humidity. It must be a cave. But why would a cave have a door?

We took a careful step forward. Daylight slipped into the entrance and I could see a little better. Shovels, hoes, parts of a plow — all covered in dust.

It looked like an old storehouse for the farmers who worked the fields.

From deep inside, I could hear water dripping.

Was this a storehouse, or a cave? I took a step inside.

"Careful, Charlie," Lázaro warned. "Let's wait until our eyes get used to the dark."

"Who do you think made this cave?"

"The water did," Lázaro said. "Mogotes are made of limestone. Didn't you read that in your guidebook? The water runs through the rock and hollows it out. But you have to be patient, because it takes forever — hundreds or thousands of years."

Lázaro liked explaining things. He was a little like my father that way.

I took another step, keeping my eyes on the ground in front of me. I didn't want to fall in a hole and disappear into the middle of the earth.

Lázaro told Delfín to wait. Then he followed behind me, but to one side, so he wouldn't block the light.

A few steps later, I came to some wooden shelves built into the rock wall. They were just like the shelves in a library. But there was one difference.

Instead of books, rifles were laid out neatly, half covered in rags.

Lázaro whistled. "I guess that's why we're not supposed to come in here."

I reached out my hand, then stopped. I remembered the crime movies on TV, where the bad guys try not to leave their fingerprints.

Lázaro came up next to me. "You're better off not touching them," he agreed.

"These guns are pretty old."

In the dimness, he counted on his fingers.

"They've been here for almost sixty years."

"These rifles have been hiding inside a mountain for sixty years? How come? Do you think they still work?"

"With a little luck, no one will have to find out."

"What does that mean?" I asked.

"It's cold in here," he said. "Let's go outside, now that we know why we weren't supposed to open the door."

I rolled the stone back in front of the door and replaced the vines that hung over it. No one could have guessed we had been inside. We walked through the fields with Delfín behind us, away from the hollow mountain.

It felt good to be back in the warm sun.

Everything was so peaceful. So why the guns?

"Ever hear of the Bay of Pigs?" Lázaro asked.

"What do pigs have to do with those guns?"

"Not pigs. The Bay of Pigs. It's a place. Some people tried to invade Cuba because they didn't like the Communist government. They thought they could get rid of the leader, Fidel Castro. They landed at the Bay of Pigs, but they didn't get far. Che Guevara helped defeat them."

"Who were those people?"

"Some were Cubans, some were Americans, and some were both. The Cuban government was afraid it would happen again, so they handed out guns to everyone they trusted to defend the country."

I remembered the shooting range in Havana. People really took things seriously here.

"When did all that happen?" I asked.

"In 1961. That's why the guns are so old. But I bet they're clean and oiled and still working."

"Do you think that might happen again?"

Lázaro laughed. "Don't worry! The only people invading Cuba now are tourists."

Pretty soon we had circled the round mountain and were back where we started, near the door to the cave.

"My family invaded," I said. I told Lázaro about what we had done in Havana. "We invaded with rolls of drawing paper and markers and books."

"That's the kind of invasion we like!" He laughed. "I do the same thing when I come here to visit. I bring all sorts of things for my father's family. Little things for the kitchen and the bathroom. And bigger things, too. They love American clothes. It's impossible to find them here."

I spotted Manzana's house as we came close to the village. My mother was standing out in front, looking at birds through her binoculars.

I heard a strange noise and turned around.

Delfín was still walking behind us, but so were five little piglets.

They seemed to be smiling, though I don't know

whether pigs can really smile. But they looked like they were enjoying themselves.

We stopped, and they crowded around our feet and pulled on my shoelaces.

I bent down and asked them, "Do you guys come from the Bay of Pigs?"

All five answered at the same time, though I didn't understand what they said.

"I don't think they do," Lázaro told me. "They come in peace."

The sun had circled around behind the mogotes. I looked across the field and saw my mother waving at me. She could see everything through her binoculars. She wasn't just looking at birds.

Lázaro and I shook hands. He had to help his father with his vegetable garden.

"Hasta luego," he said. "See you soon."

I hoped so. I'd find out a lot more about the country that way.

EIGHT
A Pig on a Bike

It turned out that the five little pigs lived with us. They belonged to Manzana, or someone in her family, and at dinner time they came running through our outdoor dining room. They hid under the table, and Manzana's son chased after them with a broom in his hand. When the pigs saw him, they disappeared between two cabins, on their way to more adventures.

"Sorry," he said shyly. "You know pigs…"

We didn't really know pigs, but we smiled back at him. Especially since the pigs were clean. People always say "a dirty pig" or "a pig sty" for a messy place, but that's not really fair. I wanted to lean over and pet them, but I knew what my mother would say about that.

There weren't really any restaurants in Viñales, so we ate at Manzana's. We shared everything with her family. It was great! Max slipped food to Monty even though Manzana told him not to. The dog followed him everywhere. I'm sure Max was thinking about a way to kidnap Monty and hide him in his backpack.

Manzana was a great cook. The food was a million times better than the rice and beans at La Roca, that refrigerator of a restaurant in Havana. When she wanted fruits or vegetables, she walked into the garden a few steps away or traded with neighbors and friends.

But there were rules even for the kind of food she could cook. She could make chicken or pork for us, but if we wanted fish, she had to go see someone in her family who had a fishing boat on the coast, not too far away. My parents told her they would be happy to go, since she had so many other things to do, but she waved her finger.

Foreigners couldn't buy fish.

That was the point of all those rules, I decided. They were there to keep Cubans and us from talking to each other.

Luckily, I had Lázaro.

The sun went down quickly after dinner. My

father wanted to do the dishes, but Manzana wouldn't let him. We took our plates to the sink, even though she told us not to.

Her daughter started to do the dishes. First she scraped some slivers of soap off a big bar that looked like a block of wood. Then she went over to the pump. She filled a pail and carried it to the sink.

That was when I saw the sink wasn't attached to a pipe. The water drained right into the garden.

Now, that was smart, though it was a lot of work.

Later, as we headed to our cabin, I spotted Manzana and her husband, son and daughter, and her daughter's baby, all gathered around the television.

Our television. They were watching a show, their eyes glued to the screen.

It must have been a comedy, judging by how often they laughed. Even the five little pigs were lined up in a row, watching the action.

I understood why my father had wanted them to keep the TV.

—•—

The next morning, we were walking down the main street. All my muscles were stiff and sore from the horse.

My father turned to me.

"Your mother and I have an idea. I'm sure you'll like it."

Max and I looked at each other. With our parents, we never knew where their ideas were going to take us, or where we would end up.

At the crossroads where the bus had dropped us off, there was a gas station. My parents walked into the little building by the pumps.

That was strange, since we didn't have a car.

As Max and I stood there waiting, I noticed a man coming up to people on the dusty street. He was carrying an open backpack over his shoulder. He would stop someone, look around quickly, then start pulling pairs of jeans out of his pack.

He must have been trying to sell them. Everyone looked interested, as if his jeans were something special.

"What's that man doing with those pants?" Max asked.

I thought of Lázaro bringing clothes for his father's family. Most of the store windows in Viñales were empty. The same thing was true in Havana. There was hardly anything on the shelves except dustballs and a few empty boxes.

Maybe the shopkeepers were waiting for deliveries, but they seemed to have been waiting a long time.

"There aren't any jeans in the stores, right?" I

said to Max. "But he's probably not allowed to sell them on his own, so he has to be careful no one sees him."

Max frowned. "I don't get it. What's wrong with selling pants?"

The pants seller moved down the street after making a sale. I was happy for him. Two gigantic water buffalo lumbered past, pulling a cart with wooden wheels. The cart was loaded with concrete blocks, and the man driving it was wearing a wide leather cowboy hat stained with sweat. The buffalo driver was smoking a cigar, and he had another one behind his ear.

Luckily, the second one wasn't lit, or his hair would have caught on fire.

Just then, my parents came walking in our direction.

"Where were you? We've been looking for you everywhere," my father said.

Right, I thought. We had just walked a few minutes down the only street in town.

"We found a rent-a-wreck," my mother added. "We're going on an expedition."

My parents wanted to get even farther off the beaten track than Manzana's cabin in the fields. To do that, they needed a car.

A few beaten-up wrecks were parked around the back of the gas station, in slightly better shape than the car with no tires or windshield in front of Señora Gloria's building.

"Look, this one is perfect," my father said happily, as if he had just found a Rolls-Royce.

He patted one of the cars. The front door was green, and the back door was beige.

Max and I climbed in. The backseat was like a heap of mashed potatoes. But I could roll down the windows, which was better than on the bus we took here.

I have been on a lot of bumpy roads in my travels, and these were not the worst. Riding on the back of Delfín was a lot rougher. The traffic was mostly of the four-legged kind (except for the chickens). Horses, water buffalo, goats, pigs, dogs and every other farm animal kept popping out of bushes, galloping across the pavement or trotting straight toward us. Some animals decided to have a siesta in the middle of the road. They were the kings of the *carretera* and they knew it. They sure kept my father's eyes open!

After dodging animals for a while, we came to Puerto Esperanza. It was a fishing port with a small fleet of boats waiting to go out to sea. One of those boats belonged to the person in Manzana's family who caught the fish that ended up on our plates.

The water was smooth and perfectly blue, but there was no beach, so we kept going, looking for a

Pirates of the Caribbean spot with sand and palm trees.

Just outside Puerto Esperanza was a crossroads. There must have been fifty people waiting there, hoping for a ride. A woman holding an umbrella was trying to organize them, but no one wanted to stay in line.

When she saw our car coming, she waved her umbrella at us. I don't think she was expecting rain, because there wasn't a cloud in the sky. It was her baton, and she was the conductor. The conductor of people waiting for rides.

"What do we do? We only have room for one person," my father said.

"And a lot of these people have animals with them," I pointed out.

"We can put the pigs in the trunk!" Max shouted. "And the dogs in the backseat with me."

But when the woman with the umbrella got a closer look at us, she shook her head. My father slowed down, but she motioned us to keep going.

An empty truck was following us. She waved her umbrella and the driver stopped. People climbed into the back of the truck at top speed, pulling each other up, helping to lift the cages of squawking chickens and boxes and bags. In no time, everyone who had been waiting was gone. The truck pulled

away down a different road than we were on, leaving a cloud of black smoke.

Our road was completely empty. There wasn't another car or truck, and hardly any animals.

In the middle of nowhere, my father hit the brakes.

"There's a sign for Playa Hermosa. I've heard of that place."

"How could you have? We've never been here before," my mother pointed out.

"*Hermosa* means beautiful. I think we should give it a try."

He turned carefully onto a rough dirt road. Parts of it were flooded. There were low palm trees here and there, with skinny cows and goats grazing underneath them.

We drove past a tiny casita, and everyone, down to the barefoot kids wearing only T-shirts, came out to stare at us.

They probably didn't get had a lot of visitors. And if anyone did come to visit, they probably showed up on horseback.

Suddenly the road was covered in smooth concrete, and it widened out like an expressway.

Why would that happen in the middle of the mud puddles and wandering goats?

I looked down the strip of cement.

We were driving on the runway of an airport.

"Look out for planes!" I told my father.

But the runway was abandoned, and so was the airport. Weeds were growing up through the cracks in the concrete. Not even a small plane could land here now. Rusty pieces of old machinery were scattered across the runway.

We stopped to take a closer look at the ghost airport.

"Look, the terminal is all boarded up," I said.

"And there's no control tower, and no radar," my father added. "They must have flown by sight."

"Not anymore," my mother said. "Someone doesn't want anyone to land here."

"Maybe pirates used this place," Max said.

"Right," I told him. "Pirates in planes."

I remembered Lázaro's story about the people who had tried to invade the country. Maybe the airport was closed and the runways blocked to keep them out.

Finally, we came to the playa.

Beaches were supposed to be happy places, but this one was a little spooky. The ruins of an old building stood back from the water, nothing but a few concrete walls and arches. Maybe it used to be a hotel, but the only guests staying there now were goats. A line of buzzards perched on posts by the walls. Buzzards were in the same family as vultures, but at least these ones weren't circling above us and making threatening noises.

We started walking along the beach. We had the place to ourselves, though we did have to share it with the wind. It was blowing so hard that the sand blasted my legs, and the seagulls had to fight to stay in the air.

"Go in, boys, and I'll take a picture!" my mother shouted.

Max and I charged into the water while our mother aimed her camera at us. We'll probably end up in a drawing in one of her books. And we won't even get paid.

All of a sudden Max started screaming and jumping up and down, like he was trying to fly out of the water.

"Help! Stingrays!"

He splashed his way back to the beach.

"One of them stung me!"

Max plopped down on the sand and started looking for the bite on his leg.

"They're not stingrays, silly! They're manta rays. They don't even have stingers."

He made such a racket that he scared them, and they swam over to me. A dozen of them surrounded me, flapping their wings softly.

Everyone was afraid of stingrays because of their poisonous tails. But the baby manta rays were like friendly puppies. They moved in groups, and they liked people.

I stood very still, and they nibbled at my feet

and ankles. It tickled a little. Some of them came in bright colors, and others were so thin I could see right through them.

"Do you see me being afraid?" I called to Max. "Come back in the water."

But he wouldn't. I stood and watched them.

There was something strange about fish flapping their wings like underwater birds. The shallow water was like an aquarium full of darting, colorful tropical fish. If you didn't make a racket the way Max did, they would swim between your feet.

Maybe they thought I was some new brand of fish food.

My parents had brought along some of last night's dinner from Manzana's kitchen, but of course they had forgotten the forks. So we got to eat with our fingers. We picnicked on a huge log, all four of us in a row. A little like the buzzards perched on another log behind us.

Far over the water, a storm was breaking. Lightning was shooting out of black clouds, but luckily, for the time being, it was going the other way.

Sometimes my father gets nervous about the weather. He kept looking up at the sky and frowning, even though the storm was going the other way. But when we finished our lunch, he announced it was time to pack up and go.

When we got back on the main road, we came

to a spot where the pavement divided in two. My father stopped and looked at the two roads suspiciously.

"I don't remember this place. Did we drive past here?"

"We must have," my mother told him. "Go left, away from the water."

"But look, the road to the right is much better. The pavement is brand new. Let's take that one."

It happens every time. When my mother says go left, my father goes right.

But he was right about one thing. The road was smooth, without a single hole or mud puddle or skinny cow. It was better than the streets where I went biking in my neighborhood back home.

But what was it doing in the middle of nowhere, and where was it going?

And then came the answer to my question.

The road widened into a large parking lot, and behind it stood a giant hotel. More like three or four hotels, separated by swimming pools and *palapas* — those huts made out of coconut branches.

"Finally!" Max shouted. "A real vacation. Let me out of this car right now!"

My mother turned to my father. "Is this really where you wanted to go?"

"Not exactly," he admitted. "But since we're here, we might as well have a look around. I'm thirsty."

My father always does that. When he makes a mistake, he pretends that it was all for the best.

My brother shot out of the car like it was on fire.

I had never been to a place like this, but I knew all about it from the kids in my class. An all-inclusive resort, it was called. There were swimming pools and exercise classes and buffet-restaurants and games and everything else you might want to do. It was an enormous playground set on the beach, and there wasn't a single ruin or skinny goat in sight.

"I'm over here!" Max called to us from poolside.

He jumped into the pool, even though we weren't staying here. And Max, being so scruffy, didn't exactly fit in. But no one was going to throw a kid out of a swimming pool, were they?

We slid into the shade of a straw hut.

"Charlie! Hey, Charlie! Why didn't you tell me you were coming here?"

I knew that voice. It belonged to Avery, a boy from my class.

He walked up to me as my parents sat down in a pair of lounge chairs.

What were the chances I would cross paths with Avery here, in a resort in Cuba?

"We just got here. See this bracelet?" Avery was wearing a green-pea-colored plastic band on his wrist. "With this, I can do anything I want."

He ran off the list of activities. The all-you-can-eat buffets, the pools, the inflatable rafts in the shape of a giant banana, the dance lessons, you name it.

Avery, taking dance lessons! In gym class, he had two left feet.

"But you know that," he told me, "since you're staying here."

"Actually, I'm not. My parents took a wrong turn."

Avery stared at me. "Then where are you staying? There's nowhere else."

I had to tell him there was. Instead of a hotel where everyone who was working there was Cuban, and all the guests were from foreign countries, I was living with a Cuban family in a cabin run by a woman named Apple and a gang of friendly piglets.

"That's impossible!" Avery said. I don't think he believed me.

I didn't know whether to feel bad because I was staying in a little cabin without even a television and eating at a table in a backyard. Or proud because I was exploring the country and had discovered a hollow mountain full of rifles with a new friend I made.

I decided my adventures were better than staying at a hotel like this. But I wasn't going to say that to Avery.

Max came running up wrapped in a huge white

towel. He squinted at Avery, then pointed at him, which wasn't very polite.

"I've seen him before!"

"This is Avery. He's a kid from school."

"I want to stay here," Max announced.

I knew he would say that.

"Don't blame you," Avery told him. "Better than living in a shack with pigs."

That was the wrong thing to say to Max. He threw the towel on a chair.

"We have our own dog, and our own banana tree. I bet you don't have a single mogote."

Avery didn't know what a mogote was, but he wasn't going to admit it. He walked away, shaking his head.

I didn't care. I would see him soon enough, back at school.

— • —

After our accidental visit to the resort, we found the road that led back home. As we were driving toward Viñales, we spotted a lady and a girl standing by the road, waving their arms to flag us down.

My father pulled over.

The girl was wearing a school uniform, and the woman must have been her grandmother. She took a long look at us. Maybe she had never seen foreigners this close up. Or maybe there was some rule

against getting in a car with them. But she decided to climb in back, and the girl sat on her lap.

My mother asked where they were going.

"Adelante," she said. Forward.

As we drove along, I stole a few glances at the girl, who must have been about Max's age. She was busy rolling the window up and down and inspecting the ashtrays. In Cuba, cars still had them. Then she leaned forward to look at the dashboard with its instrument lights, like she was in a museum.

Then, suddenly, the woman said, "Here."

My father pulled over carefully, trying not to

drop into the river that ran beside the road. The grandmother pulled herself out of the car and closed the door, leaving the girl behind.

"Señora, wait a minute!" my mother called. *"Momentito!"*

"Ask her what's going on," my father said, starting to panic.

"A dónde va?" I asked her.

She pointed down the road. *"Adelante."*

I knew that already.

"Conoce su casa." Then she leaned through the open window and kissed her granddaughter.

"Her house is farther on. She'll tell us," I told my parents.

My father pulled back onto the road. Not that he had a choice.

Meanwhile, the girl looked very happy and proud of herself. She had her own spot on the backseat.

"Cómo te llamas?" I asked her.

"Dolores," she said, and smiled. She was wearing a big bow on the top of her head like a ribbon on a birthday present.

Would my mother leave me in a stranger's car to be driven home? Never in a million years!

I could feel the wheels turning in my parents' heads. We give some people a ride — a grandmother and her granddaughter — the woman gets out of the car and we end up with a new member of the family. What if the police accused my parents of kidnapping the girl? And did I really want a new little sister?

A few minutes later, the girl told us to stop. On the side of the road, on top of a little hill, stood a cabin. When we pulled over, a woman stepped out of the cabin and waved, then started walking down the path toward the road.

"*Mamá,*" the girl said happily and jumped out.

Her mother hugged her, then fixed the bow in her hair.

"*Gracias por su ayuda,*" she said to us.

Then she invited us in for coffee. My mother said no, but I knew she did it because people here didn't have very much to share.

Dolores and her mother looked sad.

"But I'd like to have a glass of water," my father said.

Dolores and her mother smiled and waved us up the path to their cabin. The girl rushed inside to bring a chair for my mother. My father, Max and I sat on tree stumps in front of the house.

Dolores's mother came out with a tray and four glasses of water.

"From Canada?" she asked us.

We nodded.

"I have a cousin in Canada. Montreal. You know Rafael Zaldivar?"

At least this time it wasn't Vancouver, on the other side of the continent.

"I'm sorry, we don't," my mother told her. "Montreal is a big city."

"Like Viñales?"

Imagine thinking that Viñales was a big city! I wondered if people in Cuba ever traveled in their own country. Had she even been to Havana?

"Wait a minute. Rafael Zaldivar?" my father asked her. "Isn't he the piano player? I saw him at the jazz festival."

"Sí, sí!" Dolores's mother said. "He is my cousin."

"He's a fantastic musician," my father told her. "I have one of his records."

She and Dolores smiled proudly.

"In the summer, he plays in the park near where we live. I will tell him that I met you. Dolores, and..."

"Marisa," her mother said.

—•—

We dropped the car off at the gas station just before it closed. Then we headed down the main street of Viñales to Manzana's house. The street was crowded with people and horses. In front of the shops were wooden railings where you could tie up your horse.

Horses were not the only animals. A man was pushing a bicycle in our direction. Tied to the crossbar by his feet, upside down, was a small, fat pig. He was squealing his head off. I couldn't blame him.

The man didn't seem to mind the noise. He looked at me as we crossed paths and pointed to the pig.

"Su último paseo en Viñales," he said with a smile.

Poor pig! It was his last trip down main street.

I didn't tell Max.

NINE
The Getaway Horse

I was having breakfast with Max in Manzana's outdoor dining room when Lázaro rode up with Delfín, right up to the table where we were sitting. The horse had a sniff at our fruit plate.

Manzana didn't look surprised. After all, everyone was family.

But Max was afraid of the horse. He grabbed Monty and made sure the dog stayed under the table.

"That big horse is going to step on him!"

Lázaro laughed. "If Monty stays where he is, he'll be safe. Anyway, the horse and the dog are good friends."

He turned to me. "*Hola*, Charlie, you want to come with me? My father gave me the day off work. We'll have a look around, and I'll show you some new places."

Of course I wanted to go!

"I'm going, I'll be back later," I called to my parents.

My mother came out of the casita just in time to see me jump on Delfín's back.

"I didn't know you could do that," she said.

"I had a good teacher."

"What about me?" Max wailed.

Oh, no! Guess who would have to babysit Max again? I wanted to go on my own, without Max tagging along.

"We'll go on a hike," my mother told him. "We can take Monty with us."

"Great!" Max said. And he bent down and hugged the dog.

Finally, I was free. My mother could be pretty cool sometimes.

"Are you going to the Cueva del Indio?" she asked Lázaro. "I read about it in the guidebook."

He looked a little embarrassed.

"It's very nice," he said, "but everybody goes there. And it's all lit up with electric lights like an amusement park. I know another place. It's our family cave. That's what we call it."

A cloud of red dust rose up behind us as we headed across the fields.

"Is it really your family's cave?" I asked.

"There are caves everywhere. Some have a lot of visitors, and you have to pay to get in. But no one knows about this one. Just our family. And there are no rules about not going inside."

As we rode, people waved. Everyone seemed to know Lázaro. And I bet they had never seen a foreigner riding without a saddle before.

I figured we were going to a cave in a mogote, but we went past all of them, farther into the fields, where there were not many people working.

Lázaro and I didn't talk much. It was a little like riding in a car. The person in the front seat and the person in the back can't really have a conversation.

After a while we went down a slope to a riverbed. There was no river in the bed, but the ground smelled wet, and willows were growing there — a tree that likes water.

Maybe the river was hiding underground. Low cliffs rose up on both sides of our path.

"Whoa, Delfín," Lázaro said, and the horse stopped.

Lázaro jumped down and I followed. But I didn't see anything that looked like a cave.

Then Lázaro pushed aside some vines that were growing down the side of the slope. Behind them was an opening into darkness.

"Delfín," he said, "you stay here. We won't be long."

He gave his horse a carrot — a *zanahoria*, since he was a Cuban horse. To make sure he waited for us, Lázaro tied his rope to a small tree.

I followed Lázaro into the opening. The sunlight poured in, and I had no trouble seeing.

"It's easy," he said over his shoulder. "Just put your feet where I do."

We didn't have to walk far before I saw a rowboat floating on an underground river. It must have been the river that had disappeared under its bed.

"Unbelievable," I told Lázaro. "Where does it go?"

"No one has ever been to the end. We have a rule here, and for once it's a good one. We can go down the river, but we have to make sure we can see the light behind us. It's easy to get confused in a cave and lose your way out."

We took off our shoes on the dusty rocks, then climbed into the rowboat. The river was so shallow that Lázaro pushed us off with an oar.

The cave didn't have stalagmites and stalactites like other caves I've been in. But the ceiling and walls were covered in all kinds of colors, with milky green and golden streaks.

Just in case, I kept my eye on the light behind us.

It was still there.

Then the underground river widened. I looked down into the water. I could tell it was deeper.

"Here's the swimming pool," Lázaro told me.

The water was completely black, and a little spooky.

"Don't worry," he said. "I do this all the time."

He crouched in the rowboat and very carefully

slipped over the edge with a splash. Once he was in the water, he tied the boat's rope around a rock.

I couldn't very well say no to a swim.

And I was glad I didn't! The water was absolutely icy, but it felt good after the heat and dust outside. I floated on my back and breathed deeply.

Suddenly I realized I wasn't alone. Schools of small albino fish were swimming past. Above my head, bats flitted in circles. They were probably wondering what we were doing here, and why we had woken them up in the middle of the day.

"Did anyone ever live in this cave?" I asked Lázaro.

"Besides fish and bats?" He shrugged. "No one knows. We never found anything in here."

"No fires? In the old days, cavemen used to roast mammoths in caves."

"My family tried building a fire once. But we couldn't breathe because of the smoke."

"You never discovered any cave paintings?"

He laughed. "Too bad! We'd be rich."

We floated a while more until we got too cold. Lázaro climbed back into the rowboat and helped me up. My skin was all slippery from the mud in the underground river.

We rowed our way toward the light, squinting as we went. When we were finally back outside in the heat of the sun, I was glad. We lay down on some rocks to dry off.

"If there was going to be a painting in that cave back there," I said to Lázaro, "it would probably be of Che Guevara. He's everywhere. I saw a painting of him on a mountain on the way here."

Lázaro laughed. "Oh, that one. It's very ugly. But we're not allowed to say that."

"Everyone seems to love him."

"It's true, Che did a lot of good things, like making sure people could read and write. But if there was a writer he didn't like, he would put him in prison. My family in Miami hates him. So you decide."

"He wasn't Cuban, right?"

"He came from Argentina, but he ended up second-in-command to Fidel Castro. And even though Fidel was Cuban, people like Che better."

"That's weird."

"Everyone loves a hero. Che died like a soldier, fighting in the jungle. And he looked great in photographs. Like a pirate."

"What do you think?"

Lázaro shrugged. "I don't care about heroes. Though I understand people who do. They want to look up to someone. But here, most people are just trying to get along with what they have. Like my father. Like Manzana."

We got up from the rocks. The sun had dried our clothes.

— • —

We rode slowly across the fields. But instead of heading to my house, we went down the road that led to the main street, and past the pond where I met Lázaro the first time.

I was happy about that. I wasn't ready to be back with Max and my parents. I was too busy thinking about heroes, and why people needed them.

After we passed the pond, we reached the baseball field. I played a lot of ball back home, but I never arrived at a game on horseback.

Delfín wasn't the only horse tied to the backstop. Plenty of players had ridden their horses to the field.

They were warming up before their game. There were as many girls as boys on the teams.

Lázaro walked into the crowd and started talking to them. He pointed at me. I figured he was trying to convince them to let me play, even if I didn't have a glove.

Then I looked around and saw that only half of the players had gloves.

"They want to know if you've met Yasiel Puig," Lázaro told me. "I said you got his autograph. That's why they're letting you play. Otherwise you would need to sign up with the official list of players. And the guy who keeps the list is off working on his crops."

It was a good thing I knew who Yasiel Puig was, even if I had never seen him play, let alone gotten his autograph. He was an all-star outfielder who escaped Cuba to join the Major Leagues. The Dodgers at first, I think, then another team. But before he made it to the United States, he was kidnapped by gangsters who sold him to other gangsters, and he had to pay a ransom to get freed.

Luckily, baseball made him a millionaire so he could repay all the money.

I ran onto the field. *"Yasiel Puig, sí, sí, mi preferi-*

do," I called to the players who were warming up, even if it wasn't true.

One of them threw me her glove. She would play without a glove so I could have one. I didn't think that would happen at home.

Someone hit a line drive, and she caught it, no problem. She must have had leather hands.

When the inning was over, and we were sitting on the bench, she leaned over to me and said, *"Yasiel Puig, mucho dinero."*

She was right. The ballplayer probably made more money than everyone in Viñales put together. I wondered if he gave back some of it to the country he came from.

The game was tied, and it was the last inning. Lázaro was up to bat. He hit a long fly ball that I was sure was going to be a home run. All the players on our bench leapt to their feet. We were going to win!

But the left fielder on the other side ran back to the wooden fence, climbed to the top of it, stuck up his glove and caught the ball. Everyone on his team was jumping up and down.

I felt like I had just seen the next Yasiel Puig. He wasn't much older than me, but I was sure he was going to be a star.

After the game ended, Lázaro and I walked down the dirt road past the pond, leading Delfín. We were both too tired to climb onto the horse.

"That was a great play the outfielder made on you."

He shrugged. "I would rather have won the game."

Actually, it was a little hard to say which team had won. Every time one of the players had to go to work, other players would switch sides. Some played for both sides. It was that kind of game.

We stopped in front of his house.

"I'm afraid my vacation is over," Lázaro said. "I'm flying back to Miami tomorrow."

"To the place with no rules," I joked, trying to cheer him up.

He shook his head. "There are rules everywhere. You just have to know them."

"And know how to get around them," I added.

He laughed. Then his voice dropped. "All those things I said about heroes, you know, you shouldn't repeat them."

"My lips are sealed," I promised.

We swore we would meet again. In Miami, or in Montreal, or Cuba. Or all three.

There, on the dusty red road, we shook on it.

TEN
Sailing the Streets

Max and I were walking down the stone streets of a town called Trinidad when a small wooden door swung open behind an iron grill. An old lady's wrinkled face appeared.

"Cigars!" she whispered to us. "Very cheap!"

I know it's not polite to laugh, but I couldn't help myself. Imagine Max and me lighting up two fat cigars on the street. Or anywhere else for that matter.

I would have stayed in Viñales. Maybe Lázaro's father would have let me take Delfín out for a spin. Maybe I could have gotten my own machete.

But my parents had other plans, as usual. They

thought we should see a different part of the country. So here we were in the ancient town of Trinidad, where old people tried to sell cigars to kids.

While our parents were talking to the couple who was renting us a casita, Max and I slipped out to stretch our legs after the endless bus ride.

This town was the exact opposite of Viñales. There were no horses here. Instead of green fields and mogotes, there were houses made of stone with bars over the windows like a jail.

Were the bars to keep people from getting in, or getting out?

The houses were painted all kinds of sherbet colors like the ones in Havana, and the windows had no glass, just wooden shutters. Every now and then I caught a peek of what was behind the walls: patios with giant trees and brilliant red flowers.

People in Trinidad seemed to want to hide the nice things they had.

"Are we lost?" Max asked. "We're going in circles. I've seen that dog before."

He pointed to a Chihuahua staring sadly at us from a window. Then again, most of the dogs here were Chihuahuas.

A minute later I recognized our house. The iron bars were draped with socks hanging out to dry.

I went inside. My parents were still standing in the living room with Balbina and Ricardo, the two old people who owned the house. Ricardo was staring at my parents through his thick glasses, the kind a mad scientist might wear. He was wearing an old white suit and a bowtie.

Balbina was leaning on a cane, looking angry. But maybe her millions of wrinkles made her seem that way.

"We're waiting for their son, Armando," my mother explained. "He's going to show us what part of the house is ours."

The place was like a museum, but with all the lights turned off, you could hardly see anything. There was a heavy chandelier hanging from the ceiling that had cracks running in all directions. I made sure not to stand under it in case it decided to fall. Leaning against one wall were mirrors that were taller than we were.

Max and I went and stood in front of one of them.

"We look like ghosts," he told me.

I pinched his arm.

"Hey!" he yelped.

"Ghosts don't feel anything," I reminded him.

But Max was right. The mirrors were blurry and spotted with rust stains, and the glass was wavy. We looked like faded photos of ourselves.

Everything in the room seemed to weigh a ton. The furniture was dark and heavy, and the mirrors in their golden frames were like unfriendly eyes. Balbina and Ricardo looked like they had stepped out of a painting from the last century. And their house felt haunted.

Just then, Armando came in with his two children, a boy and a girl, Ronaldo and Lucia. They stayed with his parents as he led us out into the courtyard.

Finally, I could breathe. There were palm trees, climbing rosebushes, flowerpots and a well where the family must have drawn their water a hundred years ago.

Our casita was hidden behind a wall of flowers at the very end of the courtyard.

"Where did you learn English?" my mother asked Armando. "You speak so well."

"I studied. I am a doctor."

"Thank you for taking time off work to help us," she told him.

He smiled sadly. "We have more doctors than hospitals in Cuba. And more doctors than patients. So no one works every day. I had a job in a hotel restaurant, but it closed."

A doctor, working in a hotel? After all that studying?

Back home, people are always saying there aren't enough doctors to go around. Maybe Armando could come and work where we lived.

All of a sudden, we heard screaming from inside the house. Armando looked worried, and very tired.

"I am sorry. I have to go."

He disappeared into the big dark house with the ghost mirrors.

We put our bags in our casita. Max and I flipped a coin to see who had to sleep on the cot and who would get the bed. Luckily, I won.

We had to go through the dark living room again to go back outside. Ronaldo was standing in front of one of the huge stained mirrors, staring at his reflection and crying his eyes out.

He looked scared of the blurry, crying boy in the mirror, as if he didn't know who he was.

His sister was sitting on the floor playing with some marbles, as if this happened every day.

Armando was trying to calm his son.

"Ronaldo, todo bien," he whispered. "Everything will be all right."

He patted his son's arm, but Ronaldo snatched it away.

I felt like we shouldn't be watching. This was another world compared to Manzana's cheerful little house.

As soon as we were outside, Max asked, "What's the matter with Ronaldo?"

"I'm not sure," my father answered.

"Can't they give him some medicine so he feels better?"

"I don't think medicine would help," my mother said. "First they have to calm him down so he isn't so scared anymore."

Max thought about that for a while. "When I grow up, I'm going to invent some pills that will cure him."

"You have to decide," I told him, "whether you want to be a doctor for dogs, or kids."

"I could be both," said Max.

"Why not?" said my mother. "It's good to have plenty of options."

The people here didn't seem to have many options. I guess a lot depended on where you were born.

The sloping streets of Trinidad were the perfect place to sprain your ankle. The paving stones stuck up in every direction, and you had to keep your eyes on the ground and make sure not to run into anyone at the same time.

The favorite thing people liked to do here was hide. Either they hid behind the iron bars of their big windows, or they crouched behind the wooden shutters. If we passed close to them, they would pop out and try to sell us cigars, or lace curtains, or ask us if we wanted to eat in their kitchens.

Other times they watched us go by as they talked on their phones.

We were like a TV show for them.

We came to a big wide park where there was absolutely no one. And not a single tree, no shade. Just large concrete flowerpots with skinny bushes growing out of them. There were benches, but they must have been boiling hot.

But then, next to the Palace of Music, in a shady spot, I noticed some musicians wearing white suits, playing guitars and trumpets. They were gathered around an old red convertible. A girl a little older than me was sitting on the backseat in a dress the same color as the car. Her dress was spread out over the trunk and the seat, like she was the princess of the convertible.

Sure enough, she was wearing a crown and long red gloves up to her elbows.

A photographer was moving through the crowd around the car, trying to get the best shot of the girl's wide, sparkly smile. Maybe she had just won some kind of contest.

Then the car began to move, very slowly, across the burning-hot square. The crowd of people followed, cheering and clapping. The princess waved and smiled. The musicians strolled in front of the car, playing full blast, to let everyone know she was coming.

"I love a parade," my mother said.

We decided to join in. Even if we didn't know what was happening, or why this girl was dressed as a princess with a matching red convertible to go with her costume.

On the next block, the car stopped in front of a pink house with a heavy wooden door. The driver stepped out, then helped the girl climb down from the car. He led her into the house followed by the musicians, and everyone else went in behind her, shouting and singing.

The photographer turned and took our picture.

"*La quinceañera!*" he shouted happily. Her fifteenth birthday.

Then he took a few photos of us. Maybe we were part of the party after all.

— • —

We spent the rest of the day on the beach just below the town. The sun was bright and hot, and Max and I body-surfed in the waves. For lunch we ate shrimp sandwiches underneath the palm trees.

Finally, a real vacation like normal people!

Even my father didn't notice the huge black clouds mushrooming up in the sky until they blocked out the sun.

Next thing we knew, there was a tremendous thunderclap. Everyone grabbed their towels and

beach bags and ran for their cars or, like us, to the bus stop.

A dozen wet people in bathing suits squeezed into one tiny bus shelter. Some of them were carrying beach chairs and coolers. Two girls had enormous inflated dolphins. Babies were screaming. The shelter smelled like fish and sunscreen. It was raining so hard we couldn't see across the road.

Finally, the bus showed up. We all made a dash for it, dolphins included. We pushed our way into the bus, which was already jammed with passengers.

"I don't know how the driver can see," my father said, hanging tightly onto a pole inside the bus.

The windshield wipers could have been chopsticks, for all the help they were. The bus swerved and bumped along while the driver tried to see through the curtains of rain. We were packed in like sardines, which kept me from falling over. A cold, rubbery dolphin kept poking me in the face.

Suddenly the bus came to a stop as a giant wave of water washed over the hood.

"Imposible seguir conduciendo," the driver declared. *"El bus no puede nadar."*

"The bus can't swim," I told Max. "It looks like we'll have to."

By then we had reached downtown Trinidad. I knew, because when the driver opened the door, we had to jump over a river to reach the high concrete sidewalk. Everyone crowded in under balconies and porches. We were lucky to find a dry spot underneath the awning of a souvenir shop.

An old lady leaned out the doorway holding a small box.

"Cigars?" she asked my father.

"I don't smoke," he told her.

She turned to my mother. "Cigars?"

"I don't smoke, either."

The lady turned to Max and me. She sighed.

It was raining so hard that the water started coming through the awning. Lightning sizzled and thunder rolled. We took cover in the store with the cigar lady. That turned out to be a good move. A minute later, the awning collapsed under the weight of the water.

Close call!

The street in front of us had turned into a river. And it wasn't the kind of river you would want to go swimming in. Muddy water rushed down the hill at top speed. It was carrying rocks, branches and open bags of garbage. I saw a shoe go by. Then a teddy bear, a chair and one of the inflatable dolphins.

The woman from the souvenir store looked at us, then at the river. She waved her finger.

"*Muy peligroso*. Very dangerous. Don't go."

"What do we do now?" I wondered.

We were shivering in our wet bathing suits, with soaked towels over our shoulders. Max pointed to a little restaurant across the street.

"Look! I'm hungry."

"We are not crossing that dirty river," my mother decided. "The storm has to stop soon."

A flash of lightning lit up the street, followed

the next second by a deafening crash of thunder. I stared at the dry restaurant where the lucky people were gobbling up their lunches.

Then, on the other side of the street, a man sitting under the canopy of his bicycle taxi with his bare feet on the handlebars looked up from his phone.

"Señor, Señora!" he called with a big smile. "You want a ride?"

My parents laughed and waved. They thought he was joking.

He started pedaling hard toward our side of the street. Rain was pouring off his canopy that sagged under the weight of the water. He was crossing through the strong current, and I was afraid he would be swept away right before my eyes.

But he was wearing a big smile as he slowly made his way to our side of the raging torrent. He must have had strong legs.

He parked just below the sidewalk in front of the souvenir shop and helped my parents climb down into his taxi. Then he ferried them across the street as Max and I waited our turn. It had to be the shortest taxi ride in history, but the bravest.

I thought of the princess in her red dress. It was a good thing she wasn't sitting on the back of the convertible.

We returned to our casita through the tail end

of the storm. Our room was full of pots and pans and pails. They were there to catch the rain coming through the roof. But they had overflowed, and the water was ankle-deep in our room. Max's clothes were soaked.

"I told you not to leave your stuff on the floor."

Then, just like that, the rain stopped. The water quickly disappeared down the drain in the middle of the room.

Someone knocked on the door. Armando was standing there looking pale and upset. He was holding his daughter Lucia's hand.

"Have you seen Ronaldo? Is he here? We have been searching for him everywhere. He is afraid of storms. You know, the thunder…"

We looked under the beds and in the bathroom. Then I went out and stood on the steps of our little casita. I looked around the yard.

Where would I hide if I was afraid of ghost mirrors and crashing thunder?

First I looked behind the wall of flowers. Then I leaned over the well. It was covered with a metal grill. I was sure glad I didn't have to climb down there. The well was probably full of water after the storm.

Then I spotted a wooden ladder leaning against the far wall. I climbed up and saw a pigeon coop on the tiled roof.

"Ronaldo," I called softly. *"Estás aquí?"*

Everything was very quiet. All I heard were pigeons cooing.

Why would a small scared boy want to hide with birds?

But then I heard a low whimper. I crawled on my hands and knees on the slippery wet tiles and looked inside the coop that was like a small house.

Ronaldo was crouching in a corner surrounded by cooing birds. He turned his head away as if he didn't want to see me.

"Time to come out, Ronaldo. The storm is over. Nothing to be scared of."

Maybe he didn't understand the words I said, but I think he understood the sound of my voice. I wasn't sure that a boy who was afraid of his reflection in the mirror would trust me.

But then he slowly crawled toward me as I made my way backward to the ladder.

Below, Armando, Balbina, Ricardo and Lucia were looking up at us. My parents and Max were there, too, not saying a word. I climbed down the ladder first, guiding Ronaldo by holding his ankles and putting his foot on each rung, one step at a time.

When we reached the ground, his father took his hand. The boy squeezed his eyes shut as Armando led him into the house.

"*Gracias,*" Balbina said. Her lips were trembling. "You are very brave."

I didn't feel that brave. All I had done was climb up a ladder. But I was glad I could help Ronaldo.

ELEVEN
Adiós, Elvis!

Señora Gloria was on her balcony when we went to say goodbye to her and Elvis. Ledesma would be taking us to the airport soon.

My mother started describing the trip to her. Viñales, Trinidad and everything in between. And in pretty good Spanish.

Señora Gloria looked sad.

"Viñales is so pretty. I haven't been there in twenty-five years. And it's just a bus ride away."

"Why don't you go?" my mother asked.

"We can't go anywhere we want," she told her. "It's expensive. And there are problems… You have to get permission. Your Cuba and my Cuba are not the same."

Then she tried to smile. "Your Spanish is much better. When you first came, I never thought you would survive one hour in our schools."

My mother looked at me. "I had some help."

Max pointed at the dog. "Is he feeling better? He's still purple."

Señora Gloria patted the chair next to her and invited Max to sit down. Elvis came running right over.

"I think he missed you," she said as she scratched him (the dog, not my brother) behind his ears. "He kept asking me when you would come back."

Max petted him, but that wasn't good enough for my little brother. He had to give Elvis a big hug.

"You'll get better, I know you will."

The dog licked Max's face. I didn't know who should have been more disgusted — Max or the dog.

A few minutes later, Mercedes came in, followed by Ledesma. Our Cuban goodbye party was underway.

Ledesma bent over Señora Gloria's dog.

"You are the ugliest dog on the *planeta*. You are as ugly as sin. But at least you are alive."

He patted his head. The dog put out his paw and Ledesma shook it.

While my mother, Señora Gloria and Mercedes

talked about the visit to the school, my father dug around in his suitcase. He took out a plastic bag and handed it to Ledesma.

"For you," my father said.

"Un regalo," I explained.

Ledesma looked a little surprised. Then he opened the bag. Inside was a baseball glove. It was my father's old glove from a long time ago, back when he played hardball.

The glove was old, but the best gloves are worn in.

Ledesma slipped it on, then pounded the mitt with his hand, the way every player in the world does.

"Thank you. What a nice present! I don't play anymore, but my grandson will use it. And all his friends, too."

He gave my father a giant, sweaty hug.

Then it was our turn to get a present.

Mercedes had a cardboard folder. She took out some sheets of paper and spread them on the table. The kids in her class had drawn portraits of all four of us.

I recognized the artist who had drawn Max's picture. Max was absolutely enormous compared to some very small ant-people who came up to his knees. Someone else drew my father sleeping in a stone chair at the back of the garden, his mouth open and his hat over his eyes.

My mother held up her portrait. In it, her hair was going every which way like snakes having a tug-of-war. I don't think anyone in Cuba had hair like hers.

"Does it look like me?" she asked.

"Your hair is just perfect," Señora Gloria told her with a smile.

Ledesma slapped his baseball glove against his thigh and laughed. Then very quickly, he put the glove over his mouth.

"It's time to go," he said.

"Back to the winter for you," Señora Gloria added.

Mercedes gave my mother a hug.

"Come back anytime," she said. "We are waiting for you."

Cuba was a beautiful sunny island floating like a crocodile in the deep blue sea. It had banana trees and friendly horses and flowers as big as dinner plates.

But it had more than that. It was a place full of stories and secrets and rules for breaking, and life here wasn't as simple as where I lived.

Would we ever come back?

Well, why not?

And besides, part of me would always be here.

THE END

Marie-Louise Gay is a world-renowned author and illustrator of children's books. She has been nominated for the Hans Christian Andersen Award and has two Governor General's awards to her credit. She is best known for her Stella and Sam books, which have been published in more than twenty languages.

Born and raised in Chicago, David Homel is an award-winning novelist, screenwriter, journalist and translator. He is a two-time winner of the Governor General's Award for translation, and the author of thirteen novels, including *The Speaking Cure* (winner of the Hugh MacLennan Prize and the Jewish Public Library Award for fiction) and, most recently, *The Teardown*, which also won the Hugh MacLennan Prize.

Marie-Louise and David live in Montreal.

Travels with My Family

Family vacations are supposed to be something to look forward to.

Unless, that is, your parents have a habit of turning every outing into a risky proposition. By accident, of course.

So instead of dream vacations to Disney World and motels with swimming pools, Charlie's parents are always looking for that out-of-the-way destination where other tourists don't go. The result? Eating grasshoppers in Mexico, forgetting the tide schedule while collecting sand dollars off the coast of Georgia, and mistaking alligators for logs in the middle of Okefenokee Swamp.

"... it has the ring of truth for anyone who has ever been forced to spend long hours in the back seat of a car." — *Los Angeles Times*

On the Road Again!

Charlie's family is on the road again — this time to spend a year in a tiny village in southern France.

They experience the spring migration of sheep up to the mountain pastures and the annual running of the bulls (in which Charlie's father is trapped in a phone booth by a raging bull). Most of all, though, Charlie and his little brother, Max, grow fond of their new neighbors — the man who steals ducks from the local river, the neighbor's dog who sleeps right in the middle of the street, and their new friends Rachid and Ahmed, who teach them how to play soccer in the village square.

"... full of good humour ... this novel will hit a home run ..."
— *Globe and Mail*

Summer in the City

Charlie can't wait for school to be over. But he's wondering what particular vacation ordeal his parents have lined up for the family this summer. Canoeing with alligators in Okefenokee? Getting caught in the middle of a revolutionary shootout in Mexico? Perhaps another trip abroad?

Turns out, this summer the family is staying put, in their hometown — Montreal, Canada. A "staycation," his parents call it.

Charlie is doubtful at first but, ever resourceful, decides that there may be adventures to be had in his own neighborhood.

And there are. A campout in the backyard brings him in contact with more than one kind of wildlife, a sudden summer storm floods the expressway, pet-sitting gigs turn almost-disastrous, and a baseball game goes awry when various intruders storm the infield — from would-be medieval knights and an over-eager ice-cream vendor to a fly-ball-catching Doberman.

Then of course there's the business of looking after his little brother, Max, who is always a catastrophe in the making.

"An upbeat summer idyll likely to draw chuckles whether read alone or aloud." — *Kirkus Reviews*

The Traveling Circus

Charlie and his family are about to embark on a trip to another out-of-the-way place. This time they are heading to an island in Croatia, a country Charlie has never heard of.

Even for a boy who has seen the world, Croatia is a whole new experience. Sometimes it feels like a circus traveling with his parents' friends, where just packing the car is like solving the Rubik's Cube. Not to mention the stay on an island where grown men steal fish from each other and old ladies pushing wheelbarrows make off with the family's luggage.

Charlie discovers that this part of the world has a long and troubled history complicated by war, and that old feuds can divide neighbors generations later. He also finds out that you don't need to speak the same language to communicate with people — not when you're having a party in a field, dancing in the glow of car headlights.

"A salutary, unusual look at part of the world rarely seen in North American children's literature, wrapped up in family fun."
— *Kirkus Reviews*